TRAP GOD 2

Lock Down Publications and Ca$h
Presents
Trap God 2
A Novel by *Troublesome*

Lock Down Publications
Po Box 944
Stockbridge, Ga 30281

Visit our website @
www.lockdownpublications.com

Copyright 2020 Troublesome
Trap God 2

Lock Down Publications
Like our page on Facebook: Lock Down Publications @
www.facebook.com/lockdownpublications.ldp
Cover design and layout by: **Dynasty Cover Me**
Book interior design by: **Shawn Walker**
Edited by**: Jill Alicea**

Stay Connected with Us!

Text **LOCKDOWN** to 22828 to stay up-to-date with new re-
leases, sneak peaks, contests and more...
Thank you.

Submission Guideline.

Submit the first three chapters of your completed manuscript to ldpsubmissions@gmail.com, subject line: Your book's title. The manuscript must be in a .doc file and sent as an attachment. Document should be in Times New Roman, double spaced and in size 12 font. Also, provide your synopsis and full contact information. If sending multiple submissions, they must each be in a separate email.

Have a story but no way to send it electronically? You can still submit to LDP/Ca$h Presents. Send in the first three chapters, written or typed, of your completed manuscript to:

LDP: Submissions Dept
Po Box 944
Stockbridge, Ga 30281

DO NOT send original manuscript. Must be a duplicate.

Provide your synopsis and a cover letter containing your full contact information.

Thanks for considering LDP and Ca$h Presents.

Troublesome

Chapter 1

Beep…beep…beep!

The heart rate monitor connected to Tywanna beeped rapidly. Her body convulsed uncontrollably and her eyes rolled back while she lay on the gurney inside the hospital room of the intensive care unit. Immediately following the car accident she'd been involved in, paramedics arrived on the scene and then rushed her to Froedert Hospital. During the accident she had suffered a concussion, which caused her to slip into a coma, fighting for the lives of herself and the unborn child she carried.

"She needs help!" Sandra cried out urgently. She stood at Ty's bedside along with Ashley.

"Ty, please be okay," Ash said, sounding concerned.

"I'll go for help," Major told them as he hurried out to the corridor.

A moment later a doctor came rushing into the room, closely followed by a couple nurses. "Prepare the crash cart," Dr. Kraft directed one of the nurses as the other slipped an oxygen mask over Tywanna's mouth.

"Doctor, what's the matter with her?" Sandra asked frantically.

"She's going into shock."

"Will she live?" Ash wanted to know desperately.

"I wish that I could promise you that," Dr. Kraft offered as she checked the numbers on the heart rate monitor. "Will someone please get the family out of here?"

One of the nurses ushered Sandra and Ashley out into the corridor and then closed the door behind them.

Following the car accident, Sandra and the others had rushed to the hospital, waiting to be there for Tywanna. It was hard on Sandra because she felt as though the accident was her fault, since Ty had stormed out after their heated discussion. Ash couldn't bear the thought of losing another friend, and Major had concerns about how Diamond would be affected. They all hoped that Ty and the baby would pull through.

Major asked, "Did Doc say she'll be okay?"

"He...he's not sure," Ash answered blankly. "It's all my fault this happened!" Sandra cried.

"You don't mean that," Ash told her.

"No, I do. I should've never brought up my concerns with her and Diamond."

Ashley grabbed her hand in solace. "San, you never meant for anything like this to happen. Believe me, Ty knows how much you care about her, and I'm sure she wouldn't want you faultin' yourself at all." Her words were something Sandra needed to hear at that moment.

"I just hope she and the baby will be alright for the sake of her and Diamond. I don't know how Diamond will feel if anything happens to Ty and the baby. And as much as I don't care to add to Diamond's worries, he needs to know about Ty."

Major piped in, "Then I'll be sure to pay Diamond a visit first thing in mornin' and let him know."

"No. I think it's best that I be the one to let him know," San told him.

With thoughts of possibly losing yet another person close to her, Ashley couldn't seem to catch her breath. "I...I need to step outside for some fresh air," she breathed.

"I'll go wit' you." Major ushered her away.

Snow fell lazily from the black sky as it blanketed parked vehicles in the lot and the pavement. The air was frigid. Winter was in and as cold as ever. Noticing Ashley's shivers, Major took it upon himself to zip up her waist-length Prada coat to the neck. "There," he smirked. His breath frosted the air. He sensed she was bothered. "What is it, Ash?"

"It's just that I can't bear to lose anyone else close to me." Ashley wrapped her arms firmly around herself against the cold.

"Listen, let's just hope Ty will be fine."

"Major," she began hesitantly. "I also worry about losin' you. I already lost Chase to the streets. I love you, Major, and I don't want you to suffer the same fate."

"You know I love you too, Ash. As well as the twins. And I'm here for y'all," he assured her.

Ash held her eyes shut and said, "Then give up the streets."

Major fell silent. Just giving up the street life wasn't as easy as it seemed. Diamond was counting on him to hold down the streets in his absence, and Major planned to do just that, although eventually he planned to leave the streets behind.

Finally Major spoke. "Ashley, it ain't that easy. I——"

"No, Major," Ashley intervened, holding up a hand, gesturing for him to stop. "What's not easy is constantly worryin' about the one you love bein' shot dead in the streets. I don't want to have to live that way any longer, and neither should you."

"And believe me, I don't, Ash. Which is why I'm tryna get my rap career off the ground. But right now the fuckin' street life is all I have." His final sentence cut her deep.

"Then what about me and the twins, Major, huh?" She sounded hurt.

"Ash." He grabbed her hand gingerly, "I didn't mean it like that." His tone was sincerely apologetic.

Ashley withdrew her hand. "Just leave, will you?"

"Ash!" he called after her as she turned, heading back inside the hospital without allowing him an opportunity to say another word. Looking at her from behind, Major couldn't see the tears rimming her eyes.

Meanwhile, Sandra was seated in the ICU waiting area. Not knowing what was going on with Tywanna was stressful on her. Ty was her only child and she loved her dearly, and now there was also the baby Ty carried, San's grandchild. More than anything, San wanted them both to be okay.

As Ash approached, San noticed tears in her eyes. "Are you alright?" Sandra asked.

Ashley slowly nodded, fighting back her tears.

"Where's Major?"

"Told him to leave," she answered in a low voice. "I don't know if things will continue to work between us." Tears began to wet her cheeks.

San stood and wrapped Ashley in her embrace. "Aww, sweetie, don't cry. I'm sure whatever it is will work itself out. It's obviously he loves you, and you deserve that. Just like he deserves your love in return."

Ashley understood that Sandra was right. The love she shared with Major was true, and she valued it. "I really do 'preciate you comforting me, San," Ash said.

"Anytime. Girl, you're like my daughter - just as much Tywanna." The two broke their embrace.

"And have you heard anything about how Ty's doin' so far?" Ash was hoping there would be some good news.

Sandra let out a sigh of frustration. "Still nothing. I don't know how I'd deal with it if anything happens to her and the baby."

"Let's just hope for the best," Ashley encouraged.

Shortly thereafter, Dr. Kraft found them in the waiting area. The doctor proceeded towards them over the linoleum floor but judging by her face of stone, they couldn't read whether she was the bearer of good or bad news.

"How's my daughter and grandchild?" asked Sandra. All she cared to hear was they were both fine.

"Can we see them?" Ash wanted to know.

Dr. Kraft took a deep breath. "Well, due to severe shock, Tywanna went into cardiac arrest. And during that her heart failed twice, but we managed to keep her heart pumping. It did affect the fetus, sending Tywanna into premature labor. She's still comatose and hardly in stable condition, and we're left with one of two choices," she reported, maintaining her calm.

"What does that mean, Doctor?" Sandra inquired, afraid of the answer.

The doctor slowly shook her head: "I'm sorry...but it means that there's a choice to save either the mother or the child."

***

Diamond lay on the gurney, staring at the ceiling. Last he remembered was bleeding to death from the stab wounds he'd suffered before blacking out. Next thing he knew he had awakened in pain with his wounds patched up and found himself located in the county jail's infirmary. Once again he'd been fortunate enough to escape from the ominous presence of death.

Seems everyone wants me dead for some reason, he thought. Therefore he needed to dead anyone considered an enemy. First and foremost, he had to make it out of jail alive. And as soon as he got out of the infirmary he'd start by tending to Spade for shanking him and for the murder of his homeboy T-Money.

But Diamond knew that his key out of jail was the crooked Fed Lynch. It was Lynch who had set up Diamond in his attempt to convince Diamond to snitch on the mob boss Frank Balistrieri. Only thing Diamond needed was for Lynch to admit to the D.A. that he and his fellow agents had raided Diamond's place unannounced before Diamond opened fire on them. Then Diamond would be able to walk free. And with the leverage he had on Lynch, Diamond was sure that once his lawyer Levin approached the agent with the ultimatum of cooperating or being turned over to the mob boss, then Lynch would rather cooperate. However, Diamond planned to body Lynch personally once he returned to the streets.

Shit, I wouldn't even be on lock if it hadn't been for Toni trustin' that police-ass nigga Pelle, he thought seethingly. And even though Toni had deaded Pelle for his betrayal and he'd retrieved the $1.3 million she attempted running off with, Diamond couldn't let her live due to being the one who brought Pelle in. And had the Feds not raided the theater when Diamond was only a squeeze of the trigger from pulling a slug in Toni's dome, then she'd definitely be a dead bitch right now. Part of him didn't want to squeeze the trigger on her, however, it was part of the game.

And once I'm back in the streets, then I'ma let Gangsta and Banks feel my heat, Diamond swore introspectively. Both them niggas had another thing coming if they doubted he'd come after them eventually. Unbeknownst to Diamond, during the night of the raid Gangsta and Banks had separately laid on the theater, waiting to get

11

at him. But the Feds raiding the stash house prevented what would have been a three-way shootout. Diamond knew either Gangsta or Banks would murk him if given the chance because both desired to seize power over the streets he ruled. Diamond trusted that in his absence from the streets, Major would keep Gangsta and Banks in check.

Nigga reminds me of myself, Diamond thought in regards to Major. Thus far Major had proven to be the main nigga among Diamond's crew that was trustworthy, which is why Diamond had made the decision to leave Major temporarily in charge of the operation. He also left it up to Major to cover the debt owed to Balistrieri. Diamond trusted that Major had shit under control, and maybe he was even ready to permanently be the head nigga in charge while Diamond retired from the game for the sake of his family.

Damn... Tywanna and our daughter need me to be there for them, Diamond contemplated with emotion. He easily loved both his girls more than anything. In that moment, Diamond needed to know they were safe and sound in order to ease his mind.

If only he knew that wasn't true.

Chapter 2

The airplane descended to a landing at Miami International Airport. Toni along with Mateo flew first class to the Sunshine State to get away for a few days. It had been Mateo who insisted they take the trip, promising Toni she would thank him later.

Subsequent to departing the plane, Toni and Mateo made their way to baggage claim. They were approached by a husky Cuban guy with a long ponytail and pencil thin mustache and fluorescent green eyes. He rocked a yellow Gucci polo shirt with cargo shorts and Gucci loafers, plus his gold rope necklace and huge three karat diamond pinky ring couldn't go unnoticed. The Cuban guy held an air of confidence about himself.

"Welcome to Miami," the Cuban guy greeted with a Spanish accent.

Toni disdainfully eyed him and questioned, "You are..?"

"Milio! It's so nice to see you," Mateo expressed, clearly familiar with the Cuban guy. The two embraced briefly, then Mateo turned to Toni. "This is my older brother, Milio, and Milio, this is Toni, who I told you all about."

Milio gently shook her hand. "Now I see why Mateo likes you so much." He smiled, contemplating her beauty.

"Nice to meet you." Toni had never known Mateo had a brother and wondered why he didn't mention anything to her about Milio.

"How about we get outta here?" Milio told them. "No need to worry about your luggage. Just turn in your tickets and I'll arrange for it to be delivered to my place."

While back in Milwaukee there was snowfall and littered streets, Miami offered sunshine and sandy beaches. Palm trees swayed in the wind and boats bobbed in the sea. The trio drank in the scene in the scene as they cruised along with the roof down in Milio's silver Rolls Royce Phantom. They arrived in Little Havana in Miami, which was predominantly occupied by Cuban residents. Shortly thereafter, they pulled into a horseshoe-shaped driveway of a large, handsome $2.6 million mini-mansion. Parked in the driveway were also a McLaren P1 and sleek black Ducati motor bike. The lavish estate and luxury wheels were the pride of a drug boss, and apparently that was Milio.

Milio led the way inside the fortress of a home with Toni and Mateo in tow. The place was lavishly furnished. Upon entering, the floor was a sea of plush white carpet. There was a red Italian leather furniture set, matching glass tables and shelves, a massive aquarium filled with exotic sea creatures, and a few portraits of the fictional Cuban gangster Tony Montana were mounted on the walls. Not to mention there were two model-looking bitches scantily dressed lounging around.

"Make yourselves at home. Gotta make a business call," Milio told them before stepping away.

In one of the four guest rooms, Toni stood looking out the window, which had a view of the huge underground pool in the backyard. She turned to Mateo and said, "Thought we came here to Miami to get away? You never mentioned we'd be vistin' with Milio, let alone that you have a brother who's a drug boss."

"We are here to get away, baby," Mateo told her. He laid on the well-made king-sized bed. "And as for Milio, sorry I didn't mention him to you, but he prefers things that way. But after telling Milio all about you, he wanted to meet you himself. I figured since Diamond is no longer an option, then you'll need someone to supply you, and I'm sure you and Milio can be beneficial to one another."

"You expect me to just turn my back on Diamond? Well, it ain't that simple. Besides, without him I don't have an operation to move supplies on my own,"

Mateo sat up in bed. "Diamond's the one who turned his back on you, even after all you've done for him. I get that you respect Diamond, but it's time that you demand he and the others put some respect on your name," he encouraged.

"Know what? You're right. Niggas need to be shown what a bad bitch is all about." She snapped her fingers with sass for emphasis.

14

"Why don't you bring your bad ass over here and show me?" Mateo grinned.

Toni seductively walked over to the bed. She began kissing Mateo deeply and sucking on his lower lip. The two were easily aroused by each other's touch. Her pussy was wet and his dick hard. In between kisses, they helped each other out of their clothes. Mateo slipped Toni's erect nipple in his mouth, massaging it with his tongue before moving to the other while Toni set free tiny moans of pleasure. After her titties were teased for a bit, Toni turned and bent over the edge of the bed, tooting up her ass.

"Eat the booty like groceries," she told Mateo, looking back at him over her shoulder.

Dropping onto his knees, Mateo spread her ass cheeks and tongue kissed her asshole. He flicked his tongue over her rosebud while reaching around and slipping two fingers in and out of her twat.

"Mmm...yeeess, you eatin' all this ass so damn good, boy!" Toni groaned.

Mateo lapped up the juices coming from her asshole, driving her wild!

"Fuck me, Mateo, fuck me in the ass."

Mateo slid his dick deep inside her from the back, loving how tight and slippery it was. She enjoyed the feel of his hardness as Mateo moderately stroked her and she gripped the sheets, taking the dick. It turned Mateo on even more when Toni reached back in between her legs and caressed his balls.

"Dammit, babe! I-I love it so much!" Mateo grunted as he began fucking her harder.

"Oh, shit...that's it right there!" Toni moaned.

"Mmm, I can feel you comin' out the ass!" He enjoyed her asshole tightening around his dick as her juices slid down his legs. No longer able to contain the nut that swelled up in the tip of his dick, Mateo pulled out and squirted warm cum on her lower back and ass.

The two climbed into the bed panting, drained from their quickie fuck.

"I'm gonna go check on our luggage," Mateo said as he slid out of the bed. He stepped into his skinny jeans.

Toni used her elbow and hand to prop her head up. "I packed a few toys that I know you'll like," she told him.

"For you, or me?" Being sexually fluid, Mateo never minded being Toni's boy toy. He got off on her dominance.

"Depends." Toni smirked.

"Then let's hope our luggage arrived."

While Toni lay in bed, what Mateo had said earlier about being rightfully respected by Diamond and others crossed her mind. She hated that shit was complicated between her and Diamond, but she understood the rules of the game. However, Toni planned to change the game by taking over, and she knew the only way to do so she had to be down to take any muthafucka out of the game.

***

The past week had been hard on Jade. She hadn't eaten or slept much because all she could seem to do was think about Banks. After revealing to him that she'd been forced by Gangsta to take part in killing Lexi, she hoped Banks would forgive her, but instead, Banks was so livid that he was finna put a slug in her shit - until she told him she was pregnant by either Banks or Gangsta.

Jade was seated on the sofa in the front room of her apartment while on her iPhone, trolling Banks's Instagram. She'd been attempting to reach him since the night he dismissed her, but apparently, he didn't want a damn thing to do with her ass. She regretted telling him the truth about Lexi, but her guilty conscience had prompted her to. And even though Lexi had been one of her besties and Banks's girl in the past, Jade didn't let any of that prevent her from falling in love with Banks. But she was sure that now he hated her with passion. Maybe if she——

There was a rap on the front door, breaking Jade's thoughts. She placed her cell on the end table, then padded barefoot towards the door. Her hope was that it would be Banks, but pulling open the door, she instead found Gangsta.

"Long time no see," Gangsta said. He just invited himself in, making his way past Jade and entering the apartment. She shut the door behind him.

"What are you doin' here?" Jade questioned.

"Jus' wanted to see you." He shrugged out of his leather Pelle-Pelle coat and laid it over the arm of the sofa. "Been meanin' to come see you before, but shit's been hectic."

"Don't act like you couldn't have FaceTimed me, Gangsta."

"My bad, a'ight? But I told you shits been hectic in the streets," he told her, sounding annoyed. Before taking a seat on the sofa, he removed a sack of coke and his pistol from his person and set both on the coffee table. He set out two lines of coke, tooting one and offering Jade the second.

"No. I'm good." Jade was a fuckin' powder-head without a doubt. She only declined on the strength of her pregnancy.

"Cool, more for me." Gangsta tooted the second line.

Jade took a seat beside him. "What's been so hectic that you haven't had time for me?" she probed.

"Jus' been tryin' not to get smoked while I get to the bag in the streets, but niggas ain't makin' it easy. Shit, just a few days back the nigga Banks tried to smoke me, but luckily my ass had on a damn vest. Yeah, shit's hectic."

The night at the gambling spot when Gangsta had gotten hit up by Banks, out of preparation, Gangsta had worn a bulletproof vest because the last time he'd been in that same spot, a disagreement over a bet with a nigga resulted in them drawing guns. So when Banks hit him up, the impact of the slugs had merely knocked the breath out of him and caused him to black out. Gangsta was lucky to survive the harrowing ordeal.

"Enough about that," Gangsta went on. "How 'bout you go and make a nigga somethin' to eat? A sammich will do." He stood and added, "And a cup of Kool-Aid," before heading to the bathroom.

While Gangsta was in the bathroom, Jade snatched up her iPhone and dialed Banks. She knew how much Banks had it out for Gangsta and figured that if she offered up Gangsta to Banks, then Banks would forgive her and they could move on together. But what if Gangsta was actually the father of her unborn child? As long as he didn't know she was carrying his potential child, then her conniving ass was willing to claim it belonged to Banks. Her call had been immediately sent to voicemail like many times before.

Then she decided to send a text:

Banks//7:26 p.m.

I know where you can find Gangsta.

Right now he's at

Gangsta came hurrying back into the front room and angrily asked, "Why didn't you tell me, Jade?" He startled Jade, causing her to drop her cell before she could complete the text and send it. When he set the positive Clear Blue pregnancy test on the coffee table that he had found inside the medicine cabinet, Jade jumped to her feet.

"I -I wanted to wait until I saw you," she said deceptively.

"Who else knows?"

"No one," she lied. She wouldn't dare tell Gangsta that Banks also knew and could possibly be the father. As far as she knew, Gangsta wasn't even aware that she and Banks had been together and she preferred to keep it that way if she could help it.

"How far along are you?" Gangsta inquired skeptically.

Jade looked down at her bare feet, avoiding eye contact. "I'ont exactly know because I haven't been to the clinic yet." Anticipating his following question, she copped an attitude. "Lemme guess: yo' next question is gonna be is it yours. Gangsta I'ont need you or no nigga to help raise my baby, so you can——"

"Look, it ain't like that, so lose the attitude," he told her, cutting her words short. "My bad I ain't been able to be around lately due to how damn hectic the streets been and shit. But from now on, I'ma be around as much as I can for you and my seed. Ain't gon' have some other nigga playin' daddy to mine."

Hearing him say that, Jade understood she needed to figure out who was the father for the sake of the baby.

"Gangsta," she began quietly, "if you mean any of what you just said, then try not to get yourself killed in the streets." She had a change of heart about offering him to Banks.

"Trust, I got heat for Banks or any nigga who tries to kill me," Gangsta stated. Before taking a seat on the sofa, he smacked her on the ass and said, "Now take yo' ass in there and make daddy a sammich."

***

Banks checked the display of his iPhone. Banks had shut off Jade's call and immediately pressed ignore, sending her ass to voicemail. He ain't have shit to say to the bitch. Had it not been for Jade's claim of being pregnant, then he woulda burned her ass on the strength of Lexi. He didn't even know for sure whether or not she was pregnant. If she was, then he knew either he or Gangsta could be the father. Banks hated to admit that he'd grown to love Jade nearly as much as he did Lexi, and part of him wanted the child to be his, yet he had a child with Lexi. He understood Jade wasn't fully to blame for Lexi's death. Most of that belonged to Gangsta.

"Yo Banks, you gon' pass the blunt or what?" said Big Man, glancing up in the rearview mirror at Banks.

"Uh, yeah," Banks responded, losing his train of thought. After hitting the blunt once more, he went to pass it to Big Man, then it was intercepted by Ice.

"Big Man, you focused on the wrong shit," Ice commented and then puffed the blunt.

The trio slid through traffic with Big Man behind the wheel of his Cadillac Escalade while Ice rolled a shotgun. Banks took up the back seat with a Louis Vuitton tote bag filled with cash sitting on one side of him and an AR-15 on his other. They'd just wrapped up making drop-offs/pick-ups at the trap spots and were now on the way to Magic Clippers in order to turn over the proceeds to Tate.

Ice continued, "We need to focus on what da fuck we gon' do 'bout dat nigga Gangsta. Word in the street is he fucked around and survived our ambush at the gambling spot. Nigga was sportin' a vest."

"Know his ass gon' clap back hard," Big Man added. He turned down Hopkins Street. The car's wipers thudded against the snow.

"Still can't believe dat nigga walked away from that shit. Next time I'ma be sure to sleep his ass," Banks stated frustratedly. He wasn't willing to let Gangsta get away with the deaths of Lexi or his cousin Lucifer.

"Got shooters in the streets lookin' for 'im, but can't seem to find da fuck nigga," Big Man told him. "Til we get the drop on 'im, let's focus on expanding our operation."

"What's the move?" Ice wanted to know. He took a pull off the blunt, then passed it to Big Man.

"We whack Diamond's underbosses and then flood this trap spots with our work," he laid out.

"Been lookin' to bang dat pussy-ass nigga Major for a while anyway," Ice said bitterly. "And that bitch Toni can get it too."

"What about Diamond?" Big Man asked and then pulled on the blunt.

Filling his lungs with weed smoke, Banks scoffed, "If that nigga happens to make it out of lockdown, then we'll deal wit' him. You two niggas jus' be ready to put in work," he told them.

***

Frank was seated in Balistrieri's Deli accompanied by Little and Alphonse. He was awaiting Lynch in order to have a talk with him.

"I'm tellin' you, boss, there's something going on with Agent Lynch," Little was saying. "He hasn't been very useful lately. And if he's useless, then I don't see any reason to keep him around, you know what I mean?"

"Yes, I know exactly what you mean." Frank tapped ashes from his stogie into the ashtray on the table. "Al, how do you feel about the agent?" he wanted to know.

"Just give me the word and he's a goner," Alphonse replied casually.

Frank leaned back in his chair. "Alright. Let's see how this meet goes. If Agent Lynch isn't willing to comply with my demands, then he's all yours."

Lynch entered the deli. He noticed the only ones present were the mob boss and his squad of goons. He knew that the deli shop was one of Frank's many fronts to hold rendezvouses. If it was up to him, then he wouldn't even have come, but Frank had insisted they meet there. Until Lynch was able to have him offed, he had to play along.

"Give us a minute, boys," Frank told his two mobsters.

"Sure thing, boss," replied Little as he was followed by Alphonse, sliding out from the booth. They posted nearby.

"Frank," Lynch greeted him as he slid into the booth.

Frank tapped the ash from the cigar into the ashtray on the table while sharply eyeing Lynch. "Agent, why haven't I heard a damn thing from you in weeks now? Last we spoke it was pertaining to Diamond. I told you to do whatever you can in order to get him out the can."

"And I told you that was above my doing, Frank. Unfortunately, I can't just walk in the jail and demand Diamond be let out." If only Frank knew Lynch had actually been the one to arrest Diamond in the first place.

"Well, Agent, you better figure out something soon, because Diamond's valuable to me my operation. I want Diamond out sooner rather than later," Frank demanded. He leaned forward, rested his elbows on the table, and then added: "I advise you to act like your life depends on it, Agent."

Frank's threat was apparent and Lynch wouldn't take it lightly. Lynch slid out from the booth and stood. "Alright, Frank, I'll see if I can pull some strings to get Diamond out." He feigned compliance. "I'll be in touch."

As he turned for the exit, Little and Alphonse moved in, blocking Lynch's path. Once Frank nonchalantly gave the two a wave of the hand they parted, allowing Lynch to make his way out of the deli.

Frank needed Diamond out of jail in order for Diamond to pick up where he left off. Although impressed by Major for picking up the slack in Diamond's absence and covering the large debt owed, Diamond had become someone Frank respected as a mob figure. And Frank only respected those who earned it by the rules of Cosa Nostra.

Chapter 3

Diamond entered the visitation booth and instead of Tywanna, there was Sandra. He was surprised to see her and couldn't help but wonder what had prompted her to pay him a visit. Keeping a straight face he took a seat before the visitation monitor and picked up the phone receiver.

"Wasn't expectin' to see you," Diamond told her. If you came here to scorn me, then——

"No, that's not it," San interrupted him. "I'm here because of Tywanna."

"Something wrong?" he asked, concerned

San let put a sigh. "She was involved in a terrible car accident."

"What?" Diamond's heart began beating wildly. "Are she and the baby both okay?" he desperately needed to know.

San fell silent for a brief moment. "Diamond, I...I really don't know how to tell you this..."

"Tell me what San, huh?" he demanded, concern heavily setting in.

"I-I'm sorry, Diamond, but the doctor was only able to save one or the other. So I had to make the most difficult decision of my life," she told him with her voice breaking.

Diamond felt as if his heart broke in half, not wanting to imagine living without Tywanna or their daughter Treasure. In a low voice, he asked, "Who did you decide?"

"Tywanna." San witnessed the pain in his tearful eyes. "Believe me, it wasn't an easy decision for me to have to make. But I hope you can understand that Ty is still a young woman with a long life ahead of her, and the two of you have time to have another child. I know how much she loves you and you love her. You're meant to be together. So I made that decision to give you and her a second chance at life, love, and everything else in between" she expressed, hoping Diamond would understand.

"San," Diamond began through tears, "I'm sure that was a difficult decision for you, and I 'preciate you thinkin' about what's best for me and Ty. As painful as it is to lose our baby, I understand why savin' Ty was the best decision. She's always been there for me and loved me, even when she shouldn't have. I love her so much and need her in my life. Sadly, I'll never have the chance to know and bond wit' Treasure, although I'll forever keep her in my heart. I'm sure there will be another li'l one in me in Ty's future and I'll do everything I can to be there for them. I can't imagine how Ty feels about all of this, but I hope she also understands your decision."

"Well...Tywanna doesn't even know at the moment. She was left in a terrible condition from the accident and is in a coma," Sandra hesitantly revealed.

Diamond felt dazed. "A coma? How?"

"Due to a severe concussion she suffered. It caused her to fall into a coma state. Although the doctor's very confident she'll recover from it. And whenever she does, I'll be there for her." She hung her head and added, "This is all my fault"

"How can this possibly be your fault, San?"

"The night of the accident, Ty and I had a disagreement about...well, about you," she ruefully admitted. "It got a bit heated. She brought up her father and blamed me for him leaving us. Then I...I slapped her. I-I tried to apologize and stop her from going out in the snowstorm, but she didn't care to hear anything else I had to say. The next thing I know, I received a call that Ty had an accident and was in the hospital. I'm sorry about all of this, Diamond." She began weeping.

"You shouldn't fault yourself, 'cause you never meant for things to happen this way. And Tywanna didn't have the right to blame you about her dad leavin'."

"That's just it, Diamond. I only became so upset because her father didn't actually leave. He was shot to death," she revealed.

"And how come you never told Ty this, San? Don't you think she has a right to know what actually happened to her dad?"

"Of course, but I don't exactly know how to come out and tell her. When it happened, I felt she was too young to know the truth, so instead I just told her that he had to leave us. I wanted to tell her the truth once she'd gotten old to understand, but by that time I thought she had accepted her father being gone, and I didn't care to open old wounds."

Diamond shook his head. "How could you think dat a li'l girl could just accept her daddy leavin'? You have to tell the truth, no matter how painful it is," he told her.

"And I will," she assured him.

"San," Diamond began slowly, "jus' make sure you take care of Tywanna while I'm gone. I'll be home soon enough."

"Whenever you do come home, then what, Diamond?"

"Then I plan to get out the streets so I can live a normal life wit' Ty. She don't deserve for me to put her through more."

"Diamond, she needs you more than ever," Sandra told him, her tone almost pleading.

"I know. Now you should go be by her side." Diamond knew Tywanna would need him to love her more than he ever did before.

*****

Toni was out with Mateo and Milio at a popular Cuban eatery located in Little Havana. The eatery had a tropical design, giving it a vibrant feel. It was a spot which most locals frequented for its cocktails, cuisine, and entertainment, and tonight, the spot was bustling.

Milio had ordered their table chilled bottles of Rosé and chicken empanadas with side dishes for everyone. It was apparent that he was well-respected. Many people went out of the way to greet him and he politely acknowledged them, then introduced his company. If nothing else, Milio was a suave gangster.

"Hope you're enjoying yourselves," Milio said and then took a drink of Rosé from the bottle. "This is one of my favorite spots to hit up."

"It's nice," Toni replied.

Mateo stood and grabbed Toni's hand once the Caribbean band began to perform. "Dance with me," he urged.

"Why don't you dance with my two dames instead and give me a moment alone with Toni?" Milio intervened. He then gestured to his two girls, Sasha and Angel, whom he'd brought along for company.

"I've heard all about you," Milio told Toni. "It was as though Mateo was bragging," he half-joked.

"Sorry, but I can't say the same about you."

"Good. I prefer it that way."

"Then why did you wanna meet me?"

"Apparently Mateo believes you're worthy of me dealing with, and I needed to meet you personally in order to make that observation," he told her. Milio leaned back in his seat. "Tell me, Toni, what's a bad girl like yourself even doing with a good guy like my kid brother?"

Toni took a sip of Rosé from the snifter. "Mateo means a lot to me. I love him for who he is and I trust him," she answered simply.

"You know, I've been protecting Mateo all of his life. When we were kids, our parents fled with us from Cuba and Castro's regime. And as undocumented refugees, they couldn't find work, so our papa set up a small operation here in Little Havana to make enough to take care of his familia. But the operation only lasted a few short months before a rival dealer murdered our papa - blew his fuckin' brains out in front of everyone to make a point. And not long after, our mama abandoned us to be with some guy who beat her and pimped her out. This forced me to take care of myself and Mateo.

"So at fourteen, I started up selling small quantities of drugs, and before I knew it, I was in charge of my own small operations. And then just a year later, I controlled Little Havana. Eventually the same cocksucker who murdered our papa came for me. I blew his fuckin' brains out in front of everyone - including Mateo. You see, Toni, I decided to send Mateo away from this place, off to Marquette University in Milwaukee, in order to keep him away from trouble and so he can make something of himself other than a drug czar. However, it seems he found both in you."

Toni quirked her arched brow. "And what is that s'posed to mean?"

"Means I know more about you than you think I know, Toni Montana," Milio smirked. He gave Toni that moniker because he thought it fit her and admittedly, she liked the sound of it. He continued, "And that being so, I believe you and I can be of help to one another."

"I'm listenin'." She sipped her drink.

Milio leaned in, resting his elbows on the table. "There's this son of a bitch Cuban guy Ortiz who's supposed to be my hombre. But I find out from a dame he's been runnin' his damn mouth and that he's plotting to rip off three kilos of pure 'ron from me and skip town, then start up his own operation. He needs to be made out of an example for anyone else who's even thinking of plotting behind my back. And I'm enlisting you to kill him."

"Why me?" Toni inquired, not understanding his angle.

"Because those three kilos Ortiz are plotting to rip off are what I plan to give you on consignment. And you're not gonna allow him to take what's yours, now are you?" He eyed her closely.

"Ain't no nigga takin' mine - that's a promise!" Toni thought this was an opportunity which she couldn't pass on, especially since she could no longer rely on Diamond and his connect. She needed to establish her own in order to put in motion her plans to take over the game.

Toni polished off the remains of her drink. "I'll do it on one condition: you have to provide an avenue to have the supply shipped to me," she bargained.

"No problem," Milio assured her.

***

Entering the warmth of her crib, Ashley closed the door behind herself. She found Gangsta in the front room seated on the sofa. He was watching a Milwaukee Bucks game on the flat screen and eating fruit snacks. She hadn't seen his ass in over a week.

"Boy, what'chu doin' here - besides eatin' up my babies fruit snacks?" Ash said. She set her Prada purse on the stand near the front door and then shrugged out of her Prada coat before hanging it in the closet.

"A nigga can't drop by to visit his li'l sis? And where is my niece and nephew, by the way? At least they'd be happy to see me," Gangsta half-joked.

"They bad asses are by Chase's parents' place."

"And Major?" he scoffed.

"His ass is at the studio, as usual," she said, annoyed. Major spent more time at the studio than with her with her lately.

"Nigga can't even rap," Gangsta commented, shaking his head.

Ash stepped out of her snow-wet Uggs at the front door, leaving them beside Gangsta's Timberlands. "Anyway, how come I ain't seen you in a while?" she asked, taking a seat beside Gangsta.

"Had to get low for a minute," was all he offered.

"You really need to be careful in the streets, Gangsta," she told him with concern.

"I know, Ash." He didn't care to hear that shit right now, so he purposely changed the topic. "Where you comin' from?"

"Visitin' Ty in the hospital."

Gangsta looked to her with furrowed brows. "Hell she doin' in the hospital?"

"She had a bad car accident. It left her in a coma. The worst thing is she lost her and Diamond's baby." Ashley found that difficult to even say, her voice breaking with emotion.

"Ty's a soulja. She'll be a'ight," he said and wrapped his arm around her in solace. "Does Diamond know?"

"San went to visit with Diamond and told him everything. Said he took it better than expected."

"Knowin' Diamond, he ain't one to let emotions overcome him." Though he had his differences with Diamond, he felt for Diamond, especially now that he understood how good it felt having what he expected was his own child on the way with Jade.

"The real concern is how Ty's gonna take it. Whenever she finds out, I'm sure it'll be hard on her, and as her friend, I'll do my all to comfort her."

"She's fortunate to have a friend like you. And I'm sure Jade will be there to comfort her too."

Girl, you need to tell him all about Jade's hoe ass, Ashley's conscience urged. She hadn't told Gangsta about hers and Tywanna's fallout with Jade after Jade disrespected their deceased friend Lexi by unapologetically getting with Banks. And Ash recognized Gangsta had feelings for Jade, so she understood he should know all about the hoe.

"Big bro," Ash began hesitantly, "there's somethin' you should know about Jade."

"What is it?" he asked curiously.

Ash exhaled and then shifted towards him. "For starters, she's no longer me and Tywanna's friend."

Gangsta drew back, looking at her puzzled. "Since when?"

"Since we found out she's been gettin' with B——"

"Matter fact, I'ont even wanna hear 'bout whatever female drama y'all got goin' on," he interrupted in a temper and hurried to his feet.

"But Gangsta, you really should hear this!" Ash cried out.

"Naw, Ash, I'ont have to hear that shit. But if you care to hear what I have to say: Jade's pregnant wit' my baby," he told her, and Ashley nearly fell out of her seat caught by surprise.

Ash stood and told him, "You don't know if it's even yours."

"Thought you'd be happy for me and yo' friend," he breathed. He stepped over to the front door, where he pulled on his Timbs and then slid on his Pelle-Pelle.

"Gangsta," Ash called behind him as he stepped out into the winter weather, closing the door behind him. "Ugh!" she breathed, frustrated with herself that she didn't just come out and tell Gangsta all about Jade's hoe ass. And now that hoe claimed to be pregnant by Gangsta even though she had also been creeping with Banks. Ashley couldn't just let Jade get away with her conniving ways. She grabbed her iPhone out of her purse and dialed Jade.

"What's this shit about you s'posed to be pregnant by Gangsta?" Ash questioned once Jade picked up the call.

"Um, s'cuse you, little girl," Jade retorted, realizing it was Ashley. "Hell are you to be questionin' me about anything I got goin' on with Gangsta? He's a grown-ass man, and I'm sure he's capable of handlin' himself."

"You and I both know that not only you been fuckin' on Gangsta, but you've been creepin' with Banks, and Lord knows who else. So I won't let you fool my brother into believin' he's the only nigga who could have yo' ass pregnant," Ash fumed.

"It ain't like Gangsta don't have a reason to believe I'm pregnant by him. So you can stay outta this," Jade fumed in return. Call waiting beeped on Jade's end of the line. "Man, here's yo' fool-ass brother callin' now. Bye, bitch." Click.

Ashley knew she just had to tell Gangsta all about Jade's hoe ass, no matter how much he didn't want to hear it.

***

"I got bad bitches countin' money for me. I'ont need a money-counter/ With all this dirty money on me, I need a money-shower,/ If they hate, then let 'em hate and jus' watch the money pile up/ When you in the game, it's about gettin' respect, money in power..."

The beat blared through the headphones while Major was in the booth laying down a verse to his track "Money Showers" as the first single to his album, hoping the response to it would be good. Major was a serious hustler who was trying to make some legal money in the music business, using profit from his dealings in the streets to fund and promote his own projects. He'd been performing at any bar, night club, and strip joint that would let him get on the mic. These were not paid performances. A lot of the times he had to pay to perform. But over the months, he had built a following.

Major stepped out of the booth after recording the verse. "How was that?" he asked his producer Racks, who was positioned behind the elaborate keyboard panel.

"That was dope!" Racks replied. "Trust me, that's gonna be a hit record."

"Fo' sho'," Major concurred. "Let's take five so I can burn a blunt before steppin'." Major figured they were both in need of a break since he and Racks had been in the studio for the better part of the day doing music.

Standing up from behind the keyboard, Racks made his way out of the room to make a call while Major took a seat on the chocolate leather sectional beside Spirit, who passed him a rolled blunt of kush.

"Major, you ever dream about what life will be like to be rich and famous?" Spirit wanted to know. She produced a lighter and held the flames underneath the tip of the blunt.

Major's cheeks got hollow and the blunt end glowed. "Everybody dreams about a better life." He puffed the blunt.

"In your dreams, is there anyone else?" she probed.

"Well, Racks gonna handle my productions and you're gonna be an artist."

"I mean…a woman."

Before Major could respond, Spirit leaned in and kissed him on the lips and he didn't resist. Spirit then straddled his lap and began planting kisses on his neck while Major palmed her ass with his free hand. Major's dick grew hard from lust.

Can't do this shit to Ash, Major contemplated. Hell yeah he found Spirit sexy, and he was tempted to fuck her right then and there in the studio, but he loved Ashley too damn much to cheat on her. Though shit had been rocky between him and Ash due to his lifestyle, Major knew they had had something real.

"What's wrong?" Spirit inquired in between kisses on his neck. She felt Major's dick deflate.

"Can't do this to my girl," he told her.

"Jus' relax. I gotcha. She reached down and fondled Major's dick through his Versace sweatpants.

Major pushed her aside off his lap and grumbled, "Told yo' ass I can't do this, a'ight?" He stood.

Spirit sucked her teeth. "Thought there was a vibe, Major."

"Bitch, you killin' my vibe right now," he retorted.

Racks returned to the room. He peeped tension between Major and Spirit, but minded his business and sat behind the huge keyboard panel.

"Yo Racks, run that beat back," Major instructed as he made his way into the booth.

Chapter 4

In the county jail's compact conference room, Diamond took a seat across the small table from Levin.

"Are you okay, Diamond? Seem to be in some pain," Levin pointed out, noticing Diamond's ginger movements.

"Someone tried killin' me. Stabbed me several times. But I'll live." Diamond was still healing from his wounds.

"Apparently, I need to get you out of here sooner rather than later. Unfortunately, I have yet to speak with Agent Lynch. He doesn't seem to have any time for me. But rest assured that I will have him make time. "

Diamond leaned forward, resting his crossed arms on the table. "Levin, I can't stand to be in this hell hole for much longer. I need to get home to Tywanna," he said desperately.

"She alright?" Levin inquired with concern.

Diamond slowly shook his head. "She...she had a tragic car accident. It left her in a damn coma, and she...she lost our child." He choked back tears, finding it hard to speak about the tragedy.

"Diamond, I'm sorry," Levin said solemnly. "If there's anything I can do, just let me know."

"Only thing I need you to everything you can to get me the hell outta here."

"Will do. Just be patient."

"Easy for you to say!" Diamond raged and slapped down hard on the table out of frustration. "You ain't the muthafucka who has to be in here pretty much powerless to help yo' situation."

Levin sat there unraveled. "I understand you're frustrated. I need you to understand I'll do everything I can for you."

"My bad, Levin. I jus'——"

"Forget about it, Diamond," Levin told him. He set his hands on the table. Peeking out from under his cuff was the smooth, thin gold band of a Rolex. "Soon you'll return to the streets and reclaim your position of power."

***

Placing his green eye to the retinal scanner on the safe, Yul was able to gain access and its lock disengaged. His was the only eye the scanner recognized.

"Siah, put de money in de safe while me talk bidness wid Gangsta," Yul directed. He turned his crazy-colored eyes on Gangsta. "Come."

They were meeting at Yul's warehouse. Gangsta was there with Playboy dropping off the latest gains, which wasn't as much in comparison to what used to be brought in. But lately, for one reason or another, business wasn't thriving.

Gangsta along with Playboy followed Yul through the warehouse with Rasheym brought up the rear, toting an AK-47. With Yul in the lead, they entered the chilling meat locker, where there was a man stripped ass naked, beaten half to death, and dangling from a sharp hook pierced through the flesh at the nape of his neck.

"You see, Gangsta," Yul began as he slowly circled the helpless man, "dis is what happens when a blood-clot no hav' me money." He came to a halt with his back to Gangsta n'em while he eyed the half-dead man. "An' me no like dat you no makin' as much money lately." His tone was disapproving.

"Like it or not, Yul, I'm havin' trouble makin' money off the fuckin' product 'cause the damn fentanyl in the shit has junkies OD'ing, so it's slowin' down business. Not to mention due to all of the damn OD's, the laws has been snoopin'," Gangsta told him firmly.

"Not me prollem, mon. All me give a fuck 'bout is me money, so me encourage you to find a way to move mo' product. 'Cause…" Yul came off the waist with a hunting knife and plunged it deep in the man's breast, causing the man to let out a bloodcurdling scream. Yul twisted the knife and carved out the man's heart, then held up the organ in his bloody hand for Gangsta to see.

Gangsta did his all to maintain his composure at the gruesome sight, not willing to show any sign of weakness. Having a weak stomach, Playboy was doubled over retching.

"Is that some form of threat?" Gangsta questioned, glaring into Yul's crazy-colored eyes.

Yul smirked. "No; dat is an example," he stated.

"I'll get you yo' fuckin' money, even if it kills me."

"Careful what you wish for, boi."

"And once I'm done movin' the rest of the product you last fronted me, then our business is done," Gangsta told him.

He turned with Playboy right behind him and shouldered Rasheym on their way out. There was no doubt Gangsta would eventually have to murder the Mega Don Yul.

***

The sun was streaking the darkening sky with layers of crimson. Toni walked barefooted along the sandy South Beach. The extent of her disguise was oversized sunglasses and a sunhat she'd pulled low on her forehead. The red satin bikini and Burberry beach bag went along with her rose.

Toni made her way to the outside beach bar where she was expected to find her mark, Ortiz. Ortiz was known to frequent this particular location. He hung out there because it was a spot to pick up women on vacation looking to have a night of passion. She spotted Ortiz and double-checked the photo on her IPhone to be sure it was him. He was good-looking, she thought, with his baby-face, soft brown eyes to match his complexion, and long, wavy hair. He only wore a tank top with floral print swim trunks and Dolce & Gabbana sandals.

Toni stepped up to the bar and took a seat on the vacant stool beside the unsuspecting Ortiz. His attention was taken by the lissome beauty with long red wine-colored locks and a sultry smile.

"Hi, I'm Ortiz," he introduced himself.

"Nice to meet you. I'm Toni."

"Haven't see you around here before, or I would remember that smile." Ortiz grinned.

"That's because I'm from Iowa," she lied. But the rest was true enough. "I'm here on vacation to enjoy myself."

Ortiz sipped at his glass of Patron. "Can I get you anything?" He offered her a drink.

"Sex on the beach," Toni requested and then sent him a wink.

"Great choice," Ortiz smirked. He licked his lips, feeling himself fill with lust looking at her.

Before the drink was ordered, Toni stood. Without speaking, she held her hand for Ortiz. He took Toni's hand and she led him onto the beach. Toni removed the sunglasses and sunhat, placing them in the beach bag, which she tossed in the sand. The two treaded neck deep out into the cool waters of the Pacific Ocean.

"If I didn't know any better, I'd guess you got me out here to take advantage of me." Ortiz grinned while they floated in the water.

"Then your guess would be right, 'cause black girls hate to get our damn hair wet unless it's necessary," Toni told him as she pulled out a small .22 handgun from her bosom and pressed its muzzle to his chest underwater. "And by any means necessary, Milio wants you dead."

Ortiz blanched and the blood left his face at the mention of the name Milio.

The water muffled the shots. Bullets penetrated Ortiz chest at point-blank range. The heart had stopped within a beat or two of being punctured, which minimized the bleeding.

Toni swam back ashore, leaving the carcass floating face down in the ocean, swimming with the fish.

***

Treasure swayed her little legs back and forth, making the swing rise higher. She let out a happy giggle with her two pigtails bouncing about. The perfect blend of Diamond and Tywanna, Treasure was a very adorable girl.

Jumping from the swing, Treasure landed on her tiny feet. The toddler ran towards her mommy and daddy, who were both there with their arms outstretched, ready to embrace their loving daughter. She was the center of Tywanna and Diamond's world.

As Treasure came closer towards her mommy and daddy, she reached out for them. And once she jumped into their arms, then Treasure vanished into thin air.

"Treasure?" Tywanna called out faintly as she came to from her coma. Her eyes gradually opened with blurred vision. She was groggy and confused and too sore to even contemplate moving. Every single bit of her body throbbed with pain.

Sandra hurried to her. "Tywanna everything's gonna be fine," she said gingerly. In that moment, San was more grateful than she'd ever been. It had been almost a week since the accident, and San was growing more and more concerned with Ty being comatose.

Realizing she was in the hospital, flashes of the car accident crossed Tywanna's mind. Aside from her aching head and the pain that stabbed at her body, she didn't know exactly how tragic the accident had been. First thing that came to her mind was her baby. She felt at her stomach, discovering there was no longer a baby bump.

"My-my baby! Where's my baby?" Tywanna said in a small voice filled with concern.

"I'm sorry, Ty." San placed a hand gently on Ty's cheek. "The baby didn't make it."

"Nooo!" Ty faintly cried out as tears began to wet her cheeks. "I-I need to know what happened to my baby." She just couldn't believe her baby was gone.

San let out a heavy breath. "Well, after the accident, you went into premature labor and unfortunately the doctor was only able to save either you or the baby. Ty, I thought it was best to save your life," she explained with a tone of sorrow.

"No, you should have saved my baby instead," Ty sobbed. "Why didn't you save Treasure?" Hers was a tone of resentment.

"T-Tywanna, believe me, it wasn't at all an easy decision for me to have to be forced to make. I didn't want to lose either of you.

But I thought it was best because you have a lot to live for, and that includes being with Diamond," San expressed, hoping that Ty would understand her decision.

"But what about Diamond? He's gonna hate me for losin' our daughter." She raised pain-filled eyes to San.

"No, that's not true. I went to see Diamond and told him all about it and he was very understanding. He loves you no matter what, Ty." San reassured her. "Sweetie, listen——"

Doing a routine checkup, Dr. Kraft tapped on the door before entering the room. "Nice to see you finally with us." She smiled, finding her patient conscious. She checked Tywanna's pulse, put a stethoscope to her chest, and said "good" several times.

"Will she be okay?" San wanted to know.

"We've done a CT scan. She has no evidence of a skull fracture or any bleeding or contusions in or around her brain. As you know, she had a laceration of her scalp that required stitches, and she suffered a severe concussion." Dr. Kraft saw San had taken it all in and added, "We gave her some medications for her pain, though we have to be very careful with that. She's still groggy. It's hard to predict how long that will last. After the blow she had it may be hours, may be days, or even weeks."

"Doctor," Tywanna began through tears, "why couldn't you have saved me and my baby? Why?"

Dr. Kraft eyed her empathetically. "Well, from a medical standpoint, due to you going into cardiac arrest and the pressure on your heart during your premature labor, it was unlikely that we could save you both," she explained. "I'm very sorry about your child. However, you should be grateful that you're still alive."

"How can I be grateful when my baby's gone? I would rather she be alive than me."

"Don't think like that, Ty," San told her. "You'll always be able to have another baby."

"But I don't wanna another baby! I want Treasure!" Ty cried.

Dr. Kraft felt compelled to chime in. "Unfortunately," she spoke in a low voice and looked at the two sorrowfully, "the surgery to remove the fetus from the uterus more than likely caused infertility. Which means, sadly enough, you may not be able to conceive children."

The unfortunate news caused Tywanna's heart to sink like a stone in water. Ty didn't know how to feel or what to think. And up until now, Sandra hadn't even been aware that undergoing the surgery put Ty at risk of being able to conceive again. San felt sick in her heart, in her soul.

Breathing shakily, Ty said, "But if I can't have any more kids, then Diamond won't wanna be with me."

"Diamond will still want you," San assured her.

"Even if you're not able to conceive, there are always other options," Dr. Kraft mentioned.

"I wouldn't need any other options had my baby been saved instead," she sobbed.

"I-I can't imagine how you must feel right now," San said apologetically.

"No, you can't," Ty retorted in a temper. "Leave!"

"Tywanna, I——"

"Leave now!" Ty attempted to sit up in bed and a sharp excruciating pain raced through her, causing her to groan and become dizzy.

Dr. Kraft hurried to her aid, helping her lay back in bed. "Just relax. All this stress isn't good for you. The best thing for you right now is getting rest," Dr. Kraft told Tywanna. She turned to Sandra. "I think you should leave her be at least for now. Give her time to calm down. I'm sure she'll be fine."

Once Tywanna was left alone, she bawled her eyes out. She resented Sandra for not saving her baby instead, and now she might not be able to have another baby. It hurt her that she and Diamond might not be able to have another baby. It hurt that she and Diamond lost Treasure and maybe even a chance at having their own family.

Troublesome

Chapter 5

Tate moved a pawn on the chessboard. "You know, nowadays you young niggas don't think without makin' moves in the game. Back when me and yo' pops, Cash, ran the game, we did it right."

"All due respect, O.G., the game ain't shit like it was back whenever you and my pops ran it," Banks commented.

"Listen here, young'un, the game don't change; jus' the players do," Tate put him up game.

They were in the back room of Magic Clippers. Tate sat opposite of Banks at the small table playing himself in chess and the back room was busy with gamblers and dealers, like most nights at the shop.

Tate continued, "But you have potential to take over the game, Banks. Remind me a lot of yo' pops, and he one of the most notorious niggas I know."

"Too bad I never got the opportunity to know him myself," Banks said regretfully. When he was just a toddler, his father had been murdered. "Maybe one of these days you'll tell me all about him."

Tate's eyes grew cloudy with remembrance. "Banks, there's some things better left untold," he considered.

"Understood." Banks saw that Tate seemed to find it hard to talk about his father, and all Banks wanted was to know all about him.

"Listen, I wanted to see you about our efforts in gettin' rid of that cat Frank Balistrieri. Until he's out of the way, then Lynch ain't willin' to budge on makin' a better deal wit' us. Well, I let Lynch know we'll need to catch Balistrieri at the right place and now he's workin' on it. So I advise you to keep shooters on deck," Tate expounded. He moved another piece on the chess board.

"Alright," Banks answered.

"In the meantime, I need yo' crew movin' more product if we're gonna keep up wit' the supply and demand."

"We're workin' on expandin' our operation by takin' control of trap spots that belong to Diamond."

"Diamond's one of the largest 'ron suppliers in the game, so expect a war wit 'him," Tate forewarned.

Banks took it upon himself to move a rook on the chess board, putting the opposing king in checkmate. "Then it's either me or him," he stated. Once Diamond returned to the streets, then Banks would spill his blood.

Tate noticed a nigga in the back room that owed an unpaid gamble debt. Without a word, he rose to his feet. He stepped over to the pool table, where his enforcer Dub was racking up the pool balls for a game of pool with the nigga, whose name was Smooth.

"Say, Smooth how the hell you gon' be in my spot knowin' you owe me money?" Tate said casually.

Smooth looked wary. "I'll be sure to pay you yo' money, Tate" he spoke shakily.

"Damn right you will. But since yo' ass came in my spot empty handed, I want you to leave wit' somethin'." Tate looked to Dub. "Hold his hand down," he ordered. Dub grabbed a resisting Smooth's hand and pinned it to the pool table.

Tate picked up a pool stick and slammed the pool stick down on Smooth's hand with brute force, breaking it on impact. Smooth hugged his wounded hand to his chest, whimpering in pain.

"Now get da fuck outta my spot, and don't even think about comin' back unless you got my damn money. Lucky I don't kill yo' ass," Tate spat as Dub practically dragged Smooth out by the neck. Tate casually made his way back to his seat. "See, youngsta," he addressed Banks, "the game don't change."

***

It had been a week since Toni returned to the snow-shrouded streets of Milwaukee. She endeavored to start her own operation, running a small gang of her own that was well-entrenched and very dangerous. And now that she had an arrangement with Milio, her objective was to take over the drug trade in the city, even if it reduced the streets to chaos.

Toni exited the gas station. Snow was falling like a thin white veil as she headed for her Benz. She observed the Audi Quattro pull into the lot and pull to a stop at the gas pump behind her whip. And then out came Major. *Nigga don't even know I'm finna show him and the rest how a bad bitch gets down*, Toni thought with a snort. She was still seething from Diamond having the audacity to put Major in charge over her, and she planned to make Diamond regret his decision to cast her away.

As the two were headed in one another's direction, Toni slipped a hand in her Bottega Veneta shoulder bag and gripped her pistol inside, and Major buried a hand inside the pocket of his Canada Goose coat and clutched the butt of his own. There was no secret that there was bad blood between them, and if need be, then there would be bloodshed.

"I hear you been makin' moves in the dope game," Major said, breath pluming out of him.

Toni stood eyeing him through slits, thin swirling snow piling white on her waist-length chocolate mink coat. "Figured it's time that a bitch run the game," she told him.

"Cute," he snorted. "But I can't let you think you're runnin' shit."

"Afraid Diamond will regret puttin' you in charge over me?" she said bitterly.

"Toni, I earned Diamond's respect. That's why he put me in charge. Maybe had you not brought that police-ass nigga Pelle around, then shit would be different. Diamond wouldn't even be on lockdown right now."

"And I bodied Pelle's ass just so he wouldn't be able to testify against Diamond. He knows I'd never betray him," she responded firmly. "Just make sure you tell Diamond he owes me one Major."

Major humphed. "Consider the fact that Diamond hasn't ordered you dead as you and him bein' even." As Toni turned on her heels without a word and made as if to walk away, Major's voice rang out again. "I'd hate for you to end up dead in this game."

"If it's not worth dyin' for, I wouldn't be in it," she told him. With no further words, Toni proceeded towards her Benz.

***

"Please have a seat, Agent Lynch," Levin offered.

"Rather not, "Lynch declined. He was annoyed with the whole meeting, not caring to even be holding it.

"Fine by me, because I don't care to keep your company too long," Levin stated frankly. He sat behind his desk.

They were meeting in the opulent office of Levin's law firm. Levin had phoned Lynch several different times before Lynch finally agreed to meet with him.

"Why don't you cut to the chase?"

Levin leaned forward and rested his elbows on top of the ornate desk. "Let's discuss the terms of my client, shall we? Diamond remains in custody on the charge of attempted murder of a cop. Well, as his representative, I recommend that you exonerate Diamond. Admit to the D.A. that you, Agent Lynch, failed to follow protocol in announcing yourselves as law enforcers when deciding to bombard my client's home, brandishing guns, which caused my client to be in immediate fear for his life, and, I might add, offering him every right to protect himself with deadly force."

"The DEA wouldn't have raided your dammed client's safe house if he wasn't a fuckin' drug kingpin," Lynch retorted with obvious despise for Diamond.

"That's mere allegation, Agent. Must I remind you, those trumped-up charges against him were dismissed, solely based on any substantial evidence to corroborate your allegations of my client being involved in drug activities."

"And had it not been for the only witness I had willing to testify against Diamond suddenly coming up murdered, then his testimony would be all I need," Lynch replied, accusations in his words.

"How unfortunate," Levin responded smugly.

Lynch slammed his hands down on the desk and boomed, "You know Diamond's a notorious drug kingpin as much I do! I'm sure the only way he can even afford such a big-shit, fancy suit-wearing lawyer like you is through drug proceeds!" He rose to his full height. "How do you feel knowing you're involved with a damned kingpin, huh?"

Levin relaxed back in his plush chair and eyed Lynch narrowly. "No worse than you, Agent. Which brings me to my next thing: I advise you to see the D.A. and have the charge dismissed, or my client wants you to know that he certainly have a talk with Frank Balistreri." He noted the blood leave Lynch's face at the mention of the name.

Lynch understood that if Diamond talked with Frank and told him everything he knew, then Lynch's life would be in imminent danger. He needed all of the time he could in order to have Frank offed.

Finding his voice, Lynch coldly spat, "Tell Diamond this ain't over!" He turned for the door, slamming it shut behind himself.

***

Diamond and Tywanna were seeing one another for the first time since their lives had been altered by the loss of their unborn child. Two days after waking from her coma, Ty couldn't wait any longer to visit with Diamond, and Diamond needed to see Ty to know she was okay. They always had a way of making each other feel better.

"Diamond," Ty began reservedly. "I really miss you."

Diamond thought she was still beautiful even with a few scratches on her face. "And a nigga misses you more than you know, Ty. How are you?" Diamond's voice was soothing.

"Well, my head isn't in pain, thanks to Vicodin. But I would be better if you were home with me." She sighed deeply.

"Listen, I wanna be there wit'chu so trust me, I'm doin' every-thing I can. And when I do come home——"

That's the fuckin' problem, Diamond. I needed you home ever since you been in there," Ty cut him short in a temper. "And maybe had you been home with me, then I wouldn't have lost our baby..."Her words trailed off as tears trekked down her cheeks.

Diamond fell mute for a moment. "Didn't ever think you'd blame me for losin' the baby. Tywanna, don't you realize I'm affected by that shit jus' as much as you are? I think about what if I had been there wit'chu all the damn time. And you're right, maybe then you wouldna lost her. Although what we didn't lose is each other, and Treasure will forever will forever have a place in our hearts," he expressed in a demure manner.

"I'm tryin' to understand that, Diamond, really I am. But I just can't seem to get over how much I wanted to have Treasure with you. And I know havin' her woulda made you the happiest man in the world. I wish my mama woulda saved our baby instead. Now Treasure will never know what it's like to live, to laugh, to love. So it's hard for me to live with takin' our daughter's place in this world." She wept resentfully.

"Ty, of course havin' Treasure woulda made me happy, but havin' you also makes a nigga feel that way. You should be grateful that yo' mother thought it was best to give us a second chance to be together. Listen, it's unfortunate our daughter's no longer wit' us, but no one is to blame for it, especially not you." Diamond wanted her to understand they still had one another after all.

Tywanna sniffled. "It's just all of this is very overwhelming and difficult to deal with. You don't know what it's like for me as a woman to lose my first and only baby."

"You're right, I can't even imagine what it's like for you. Although as a man it's also hard on me to deal wit' the loss of what woulda been my first-born. All I want more than anything is to have a family wit' you. And when I come home, I plan to retire from the game to be wit' you and focus on havin' the family we deserve," Diamond expressed.

Tywanna hung her head. She didn't know how to tell him that she might not be able to conceive. Her concern was that Diamond wouldn't desire her anymore because she knew that a family with her. And it destroyed Ty knowing that she may not be able to give him that. Her heart was torn from the thought of it.

Diamond's eyebrows knitted, knowing Ty had something on her mind. "What is it, Ty?" he inquired in a low voice, almost afraid to hear the answer.

Tywanna raised her head and looked at him with tormented eyes. "Diamond, I…I may... I may not be able to... I may not be able to…" Her words seemed caught in her throat. She couldn't bring herself to tell him she may not be able to have any more children.

"What, Ty?" he urged her, desperately wanting to know.

Tywanna abruptly stood. "I-I need some time to think," she said, sounding distraught.

"Think about what?" he asked, puzzled.

"Everything, Diamond. Just know I still love you," she told him through tears.

"Tywanna wait!" Diamond called after her as she stormed out from the visitation booth, disappearing from the monitor and leaving him sitting there.

Troublesome

Chapter 6

Gangsta chambered a shell in his Glock. He along with Playboy had just pulled to the curb in his G-Wagon and parked before the Jamaica Inn bar. Gangsta was there to meet with Yul in order to make his final payout on the drug debt. He definitely understood that once his business was officially done with Yul, then they would undoubtedly become enemies, and Gangsta was prepared to pop off.

"I'ont trust this muthafucka. He try me, I'ma pop his ass," Gangsta told Playboy.

"Sure you wanna go through wit' this shit?" Playboy asked, second-guessing the idea of cutting off Yul as a connect.

Gangsta hit him with a stale look like "Yeah, nigga, I'm sure." He crammed the Glock on his waist. "Now grab that duffle out the back seat and let's do this."

Inside the bar, reggae tunes and ganja smoke both filled the atmosphere. All eyes seemed to be focused on the two Yanks as Gangsta, trailed by Playboy, made their way towards the rear of the place, where Yul occupied a table. Gangsta peeped Siah and Rasheym posted nearby wearing mean mugs.

Yul knocked back a shot of Jamaican rum. "Take a seat, boi, an' hav' a drink."

"No need. I'm jus' here to make my final payout," Gangsta told him. He gave Playboy a nod, and then Playboy set the duffle on the table in front of Yul.

Yul casually unzipped the duffle, finding numerous stacks of cash inside. He didn't seem impressed. He grabbed the bottle of rum, then poured himself another shot and said, "Me wan' give you de opportunity to reconsider you position." He put back the shot and then glared at Gangsta.

"You have yo' damn paper, Yul. Now consider our business done," he said firmly.

"Me always admired you arrogance. But you fail to realize dat arrogance will take down even de mightiest of mon." Yul's threat was indirect.

"You know, Diamond was right about yo' ass. It was never a good idea to conduct business wit' you," Gangsta spat.

Yul shot to his feet and roared, "Dat's you prollem! You nothin' wid'out Diamond! Me dead you both."

With no hesitation, Gangsta came off the waist and leveled his Glock on Yul. Instantly, Siah and Rasheym drew their machinery on both Yanks. It had become a tense situation real quick.

"Try me," Gangsta growled, glaring at Yul.

"G'wan, botty mon, pull de trigga," Yul dared him in a gruff voice.

Playboy piped in, "Yul, you got the money. Now we 'bout to be out."

Gangsta swept his burner around the place as he and Playboy back-peddled towards the exit while Siah and Rasheym held aim on them. Once Gangsta and Playboy departed the bar, then Siah and Rasheym began to go after them until the Rastas were halted by Yul.

"Leave dem," Yul ordered. He sat and took a drink of the rum from the bottle. "No worries, dreadlocks, us will mummify de blood clot."

***

The digital clock glowing in the dark next to Ashley's iPhone on the nightstand at her bedside told her it was nearly two in the morning as she heard Major entering the crib. She was in the bedroom in the king-sized bed, unable to fall asleep and awaiting him.

After pulling off his Canada Goose coat and snow covered Eastland duck-boots, both of which he left at the front door, Major then made his way into the bedroom, trying not to make too much noise so as not to wake Ashley. He didn't realize that she was already awake until she clicked the bedside lamp on.

"Didn't think you'd still be up," Major said as he set his keys and iPhone on his bedside nightstand.

Ash sat back up against the headboard. "Couldn't sleep," she responded, observing him peel off his shirt.

"Everything a'ight?" Major sat on edge of the bed.

"Major," she began quietly, "ever since you started to focus on your rap career, you been comin' home later by the day and I been seein' less of you because you're either at the studio or out doin' a show - when you ain't runnin' the streets."

"Ash, you know I'm chasin' my dream. And I got a real shot at makin' it come true. My bad if I ain't able to be up under you all damn day," he fumed.

"I ain't sayin' you should be up under me all day, although I would love for you to show me some damn attention," she fumed.

"I thought you support my dreams, Ash."

She let out a sigh. "Of course I do. But at times, it seems you don't know if you care more about your rap dreams or street dreams. Whichever, I refuse to come second to either," she let him know.

Major stood and said, "Let's jus' drop it, a'ight?" He headed into the adjacent bathroom.

While showering, Major couldn't help but think about what Ash had said and knew she made a valid point. Between him living the street life while pursuing a rap career, he was walking a thin line. And he realized to become the successful rap star he had the potential to be, then he would have to get out of the streets. So he would. And he hated that Ash felt like he made more time for rapping and the streets than he did for her. He had to admit that they didn't see much of each other as of late, although it wasn't on purpose. There was no doubt he absolutely loved Ash, and he didn't want anything to come between them.

Major turned off the shower and then toweled himself dry before pulling on some Ralph Lauren boxer-briefs. After taking care of his nine, Major returned to the bedroom, where he found the lamp was now off. He slid into bed beside Ashley beneath the satin sheets. And even though Ash had her back towards him, he could tell that she was not only still awake, but was weeping, judging by the quiet sounds of her sniffles. Knowing that she wept tore him up on the inside. Major was sure Ash didn't care to speak with him in that moment, given the earlier exchange.

He reached over and grabbed his iPhone from the nightstand then sent her a text. Once her own iPhone buzzed, Ash grabbed it and then checked the message:

Major// 2:06 a.m.
I'ont want us to go to bed mad...

Ashley sent him a text in response.

Ash//2:08 a.m.
Neither do I.

Major//2:09 a.m.

U were right. I need to make more time for us. I'ont want my rap dream to come between us.

Ash//2:11 a.m.
I really do support u, even if all u had was a dollar & a dream. I would ride w/U.

Major//2:11a.m.
I ♡ U.

Ash//2:12a.m.
I ♡U 2.

Major set his iPhone on the nightstand and then rolled over and wrapped his arms around Ash, spooning her. Ash loved the feel of melting into his hold as she kissed him over her shoulder and he caress her small titties. Without words, they tugged and pulled their underwear off, and while they lay on their sides, Ash reached behind her, taking hold of Major's hardness. She thrust him inside her wet-shot, arching her back for him. Major planted small kisses on the nape of her neck as he slowly slid his dick back and forth in her pussy.

"Mmm, yes, Major," Ash softly moaned, feeling his dick dig deep in her. She reached back and held the back of his head in one hand. "Oooh, boy. You so deep in it!"

Major was enjoying how gushy the pussy had gotten. He grabbed Ashley's leg and lifted it, allowing him more access to slide every inch of his joint inside her slick twat. "Damn, dis pussy ready," he grunted as he dug in her.

"Yes, baby, yes, baby, yes, baby, gimme dat big dick!" Ash felt him hitting her G-spot. Her pussy tightened around his dick as Major rapidly thrust deep inside her body. Her pussy oozed cum.

"Ooh shit!" Major felt her cream on his dick. It was warm and he couldn't resist the thought of tasting her. Just thinking of Ash's pussy in his mouth made him bust a nut. "Now lemme taste it," he crooned

"Mm-kay," she purred. Rolling over on top of him, she scrambled up to the head of the bed, taking hold of his head and guiding it between her legs. Major complied willingly, moving closer to her wet-wet, and sucked her into his mouth. "Unh...yaaas, baby! Yaaas!" Her moans echoed throughout the bedroom.

While she rode his face, Major sucked on her pearl-tongue and finger-fucked her slit. He palmed her ass, pulling her twat more onto his mouth, and flicked his tongue around inside her. She rocked her hips while he sucked and slurped at her wetness. She tossed her head back, loving the feel of his aggressive tongue.

"Ahhhhh!" Ash screamed in utter pleasure as orgasm racked her body. And as her wet-shot oozed, Major lapped up her juices. She rolled onto her back in the bed, panting. Major prowled his tongue deep into her mouth, allowing her to taste her own juices as his arms enveloped her, pressing her close.

The two fell into a sex-induced slumber.

***

Toni entered the bar of the Patowa Toni Hotel & Casino. Toni scanned the place, finding Tywanna seated at a two-person bar table. The two hadn't seen or spoken to one another since they had been on lockdown together. So Toni found it random when she received a text from Ty to meet with her. Ty needed someone to talk to. She had Ashley, of course, but needed someone she felt would unapologetically tell her like it is.

"Came as soon as I could," Toni said as she approached Ty. She shrugged out of her fur coat and hung it off back of the stool chair before taking a seat. She noticed Ty's hair was stylishly short. "Lovin' the new 'do, looks good on you." She also noticed signs of recent tears.

"Thanks." Ty took a drink from her glass of Remy. "Care for a drink?" she offered.

"I'm good. And maybe you shouldn't be drinkin' either, Ty. It's only afternoon," Toni pointed out.

"It's okay. I Ubered here. Besides, girl, I need a drink right about now. I'm goin' through it," Ty told her. She fished inside her Dooney & Burke bag on the table, coming out with a pill bottle of Vicodin that was prescribed by her doctor. And even though a pink sticker on the pill bottle counseled against consuming alcoholic beverages while taking the painkiller, Ty popped a tablet, chasing it down with a drink of Remy. Fuck it. She had no intention of driving a car in the next several hours.

"And what are those?" Toni questioned as Ty returned the pill bottle inside her bag.

"Vicodin, for my head. Recently I was in a bad car accident," she said in a depressed tone.

"I assume that's how you those scratches on yo' face." Toni examined the damage then added, "Boo, you're still gorgeous. In time, those scratches won't even be noticeable. How bad could the accident have been?"

Ty hung her head. She peered down into her partially-filled glass of Remy. Toni could see that Ty was tormented by something more than she was aware of. And as a friend, Toni cared to be there for Ty.

"Girl, is everything alright? And don't you think you shouldn't be drinkin' and takin' Vicodin while you're pregnant?" Toni gingerly asked out of concern.

54

Ty raised tearful eyes and said, "I...I lost the baby." Her voice was shaky. It hurt more every time for her to say it aloud.

Toni copped a hand over her mouth in disbelief and gasped. "No," she responded softly, it being all she could find to say in that moment. She couldn't see from her seat that Ty no longer had the baby bump. "Ty, I didn't know. How?"

"Almost two weeks ago I had a fight with my mom over my relationship with Diamond, and after enough of it, I packed my things then left. While I was on the expressway durin' a snowstorm, I lost control of the car and crashed. Apparently I hit my head so hard I fell into a coma. Next thing I know, some days later I woke up in the hospital. Then I learned the worst news of my life: that my baby was gone. Tears were profusely streaming down Tywanna's cheeks.

Toni could see how much it was eating Ty up to reminisce about the turn of events. She couldn't help but think about how Diamond must feel, knowing he was very proud of becoming a father.

"I'm so sorry about you and Diamond's baby, Ty. Although fortunately you're still here," Toni said.

Ty slowly shook her head. "But it could be my baby instead, Toni."

"What do you mean?" she asked, perplexed.

"Due to medical complications, I went into premature labor, and the doctor wasn't able to save me and the baby. So my mom was given the direction to only save one of us, and she decided on me," Ty sobbed. "She shoulda decided my baby!" she added, upset.

"I'm sure yo' mama had a good reason why she believed savin' you was the best decision."

"What was best woulda been for her to make the decision to save me and Diamond's only child."

"Ty, I'm sure Diamond would love to make another baby with you." Toni offered a small smile, trying to lighten up the mood.

Ty hesitated before, in a low voice, saying, "I'm sure too. Only problem is, I was told that I may never be able to conceive anymore children..." Her voice trailed off and she mutely wept.

Toni shook her head in disbelief. "I can't even imagine how you must feel," she commented.

"If I'm being honest, I feel like less of a woman," Ty told her through tears.

"Ty, havin' a baby does not make you more or less of a woman." Toni used a napkin to dab away Ty's tears.

"Tell me, Toni, what man wants a woman who can't have his baby? Certainly not Diamond. He wants to have a family with me more than anything," Ty cried.

It was hard for Toni to see her in such state. "Trust, Ty, Diamond loves you too much to let anything prevent him from ever wanting you."

"I-I'm just not so sure."

"Does he know about any of this?"

Tywanna peered down into her glass again. "When I visited him, I talked with him about me losin' the baby, yes. And he took it better than I expected. But I just couldn't bring myself to tell him that I may not be able have kids." Her voice was close to a whisper.

"You have to tell Diamond," Toni urged.

"I will. I-I just don't know how, especially seein' how happy it made him when I was gonna have his daughter. I'm afraid about how Diamond's gonna feel about me when he learns I may not be able to give him a family." Ty broke down into tears again.

Reaching over the table, Toni took Ty's hand in hers and found her tearful eyes. "Diamond will love you through this. He's a good nigga like that. And you're a good bitch, and Diamond knows bitches ain't got shit on you."

"I hope you're right." She sniffled.

"I'm sure I speak for many others when I say I hate that you and Diamond lost the baby.

"Well, I'm sure that hoe Jade would love that we lost our daughter. Especially since Ash told me Jade's claimin' to be pregnant," Ty commented in a tone of disgust. She polished off her glass of Remy.

"Mmm, and I bet her dirty ass don't even know who her baby daddy is," Toni added.

"In between her fuckin' Gangsta and Banks and Lord knows whoever else, the daddy could be anyone. Ugh, I can't believe I lost my baby and now Jade's claimin' she's pregnant. She don't deserve a baby after all the shit she's done." Tywanna shook her head.

"Trust, she'll get hers one way or another. But for now, you just need to take care of yourself and be there for Diamond," Toni told her.

"Toni, I 'preciate you bein' here for me."

"Actually, I'm glad you texted. I thought about you a lot since the last time I saw you when we were in orange jumpers." She gently caressed Ty's hand. "I mean…hopin' you were fine."

Ty found herself blushing. She shyly withdrew her hand and said, "I never got the chance to properly thank you for lookin' after me in there. It meant a lot."

"Was just showin' my loyalty to Diamond 'cause I know it's what he woulda wanted me to do."

"Well, I thought I'd show my 'preciation by helpin' you get out of there. So I paid ten bands to Levin, the attorney workin' Diamond's case, to do whatever he could for you. I'm glad he was able to get you released."

Toni arched eyebrows knitted. "What, you had somethin' to do with me bein' released? Tywanna, I'ont know how to thank you. I'll get the money back to you as——"

"No," Ty stopped her short. "I did it on the strength of yo' loyalty to Diamond."

Toni leaned back in her chair and took a deep breath. "Ty, I think you should know that Diamond wants nothin' to do with me," she admitted.

"But why, Toni? You two been down for each other for too long." Ty wasn't expecting to hear that.

"'Cause I was the one who fucked around and introduced him to the nigga that snitched on him," she answered. "But, Ty, I swear that I didn't know the nigga was a damn snitch. I would never purposely do some fucked-up shit like that to Diamond," she added quickly. Leaning forward, in a lowered voice, she told Ty, "I even bodied the snitch-ass nigga to prove it to Diamond. And he still turned his back on me." Now her eyes were rimmed with tears.

Ty could tell she was genuinely hurt. "I believe you, Toni," Tywanna told her. "And I'm sure Diamond does, too. I'd guess that it's just hard for him to get over while he has to be on lockdown."

"It only there was somethin' more I could do to help Diamond get outta of there."

Don't worry. Levin's on top of it. Diamond will be out sooner than expected. I just wonder how things will be whenever he gets out."

When Diamond gets out, Toni mused, *nobody's gonna be safe.* She was aware that Diamond would return to the streets with a vengeance.

***

Diamond was alone in the cell seated on the lower bunk, looking through his photos. He had a lot on his mind after going through some shit, from his niggas to his bitch.

Ever since last seeing and talking with Ty, he didn't much know what to think or how to feel. Apparently there was something more bothering Ty, but she had stormed out of the visit with whatever it was still on her mind. All he could do was give her the time she needed. He couldn't stand the thought of Ty being so hurt and down on himself after losing their baby. Diamond knew she cared to have a family with him more than anything, and he definitely wanted to give her that.

Shifting through the photos, he came upon one of her and his original crew: Gangsta, Toni, and Chase. The photo reminded him of a time when they were all close friends, willing to die for one another. Now they were frenemies. Gangsta had betrayed him and Toni broke his trust, and as much as Diamond hated to do it, he had no choice but to body them. Given the chance, he knew they would do the same to him. Chase had to be rolling over in his grave knowing that they were all willing to kill one another. When he got out, then he'd be sure to visit Chase's gravesite in hopes of finding a peace of mind.

Diamond just wanted to be back in the streets.

"Ay, Diamond!" Spook called out, ducking his hand into the cell. He broke Diamond's thoughts. "We bought some time to move on that bitch-ass nigga Spade."

Diamond stood and said, "Then let's move."

After having spent several days in the infirmary recovering from being shanked by Spade, Diamond had returned back to the pod. He hadn't fully recovered just yet. Therefore, for security purposes, he'd requested to be celled up with Spook, who was one of several niggas on the pod from Diamond's crew. Diamond, along with others from his crew, Spook, O, and AB, made their way through the crowded and noisy dayroom towards Spade's cell while Lil G, Humpty, Greazy, and Finesse were on the lookout. Other inmates occupied the dayroom, seated at the tables playing cards or dominoes or watching TV. Diamond n'em wouldn't have to worry about C.O. Blake sounding her alarm since she'd been compensated generously to turn a blind eye on the event that was finna take place.

Diamond barged into the cell with his crew close behind, catching Spade off-guard while he was seated on the steel toilet/sink with his orange pants down around his ankles as he was taking a shit.

"Fuck is thi——"

Whop!

"Shut da fuck up, bitch nigga," Diamond growled.

He'd taken off on Spade, who'd attempted to scramble to his feet and pull up his pants in order to put up a fight, but Diamond's blow square on the nose forced Spade to fall back down to the seated position on the toilet with his pants only halfway up. Immediately, the others began to attack Spade, flooding him with fists, beating him bloody. Diamond instructed his boys to position Spade's bitch ass facing the toilet/sink on his knees.

"Bitch-ass nigga, you shoulda finished me. This for T-Money!" Diamond hissed.

He palmed the back of Spade's skull and forced him facedown into the shitty toilet bowl water. Spade caused water to splash about and let out muffled cries for help as he suffered being drowned. Diamond stuffed Spade's head deeper into the water, ensuring he couldn't breathe.

Moments later, Spade's body went as limp as a wet noddle. Then Diamond and the others left the corpse to be discovered by the C.O. during count time while positioned on its knees, face submerged in the shitty toilet bowl water, drowned to death.

Chapter 7

"I'm finna come, boo," Toni cooed seductively.

Mateo was turned on, his dick hard. He could barely contain himself as precum seeped from the tip of his dick. Toni had a way of sending him into sexual overdrive. He enjoyed her dominance and being her boy toy. Just imagining Toni cumming in his mouth drove Mateo wild!

Toni emerged from the fitting room of Victoria's Secret. She was slayin' it in a purple lace French-cut lingerie set and white patent leather Christian Louboutin stilettos. Mateo was on the edge of his seat while Toni modeled the lingerie before him. She twerked, offering him a good look at her snatched body. Her ass and titties were perfectly shaped.

"You like?" Toni smiled, standing with manicured hands on her curvy hips. Mateo nodded excitedly. "Then later on you can wear it for me," she told him with a grin.

Toni noticed Jade enter the boutique. *This hoe got some nerve to be walkin' around shoppin' and shit, like her ass ain't done a damn thang wrong*, Toni mused bitterly. She disliked Jade mainly because the hoe had put everyone around her in grave danger and carried on as if it was nothing. Toni wouldn't mind bodyin' the conniving-ass hoe.

"Stay," Toni commanded Mateo before heading towards Jade, who was holding to her frame a sexy-ass black sheer lingerie set, examining it.

"Girl, I think that set will look good on you," she commented as she approached Jade.

Jade gave Toni a once over, admiring her in the set she wore. "You doin' it in that set, and those Loubou's are poppin'. With a bangin'-ass body like yours, you can make some serious coins strippin'."

"I'ont knock no bitch for doin' whatever's necessary to secure a bag, although I ain't about that stripper life. It takes a certain type a bitch to work such a cutthroat gig. You should know," Toni insinuated.

"A bitch gotta do what a bitch gotta do, right?" Jade replied shamelessly. "But I ain't been strippin' since before Red Velvet was closed down. I'm tryna put that behind me now," she added.

Toni chuckled. "Bitch, it's too late for that now. Do you really think you can put all of the drama you was part of behind you without havin' to watch yo' damn back?" The question was more of a statement.

"What'cha talkin' 'bout, Toni?" Jade feigned ignorance.

"Miss me with the ignorant act. I know you had a part in a lot of the drama. When Ty mentioned certain shit to me about you, it all started to make sense."

"Ty don't know a damn thing," Jade shot back.

"Apparently she knows that you been puttin' peoples' lives in danger - especially Diamond's. In between you creepin' with Gangsta and Banks, shit makes sense that you set up Diamond for them. By the way, I heard you claim to be pregnant and don't even know if it's by Gangsta or Banks." Toni shook her head. "That's a damn shame."

"Lemme guess: you heard that from Ty also. Well, I heard she lost her baby, so her ass just hatin'," Jade replied spitefully.

Toni pointed her trigger finger on Jade's face. "Nothin'-ass hoe, watch yo' damn mouth! And lucky for you I'ont owe Diamond no loyalty anymore, or I'd body yo' ass." She nudged Jade's forehead with every syllable. Toni then grabbed the lingerie set from Jade's hand and said, "On second thought, this will look better on me." She turned with no more words, heading back to the fitting room.

Can't stand Ty's ass, Jade mused seethingly. *Bitch needs to mind her own fuckin' business.* Jade had to do something about Tywanna.

By the time Toni stepped out of the fitting room, now wearing the lingerie set she took from Jade, she noticed Jade had disappeared from the boutique. Toni knew that once Diamond learn Jade had a part in having him set up, then he'd murder her. If Jade knew what was good for her, Toni reflected, then the hoe would disappear for good!

Mateo bit down on his lower lip as Toni struck a sexy-ass pose for him. She stepped halfway into the fitting room and used her index finger to coax Mateo to follow her inside the fitting room. She began seductively removing her bra before turning and peering back at him over her shoulder as she slowly pulled down the boy shorts. Mateo pulled out his erect dick, stroking it in his hand while enjoying Toni's strip-tease. Taking hold of Mateo's dick, Toni guided it inside her wet pussy as she straddled the chair.

"Damn, boy! Mmm, yes," Toni moaned softly, pouncing on Mateo's hardness.

He moved his lips to meet her open mouth, taking small, gentle bites of her lower lips, as his hand palmed her ass. Mateo then took her titty into his mouth, sucking on her erect nipple, and Toni dug her nails into his shoulders out of pleasure. She tip-drilled his dick, sliding her pussy up to its tip and slamming down on it, hitting her G-spot each time.

"Ohhh shiiit, yes! I'm cummin'!"

Toni tossed her head back as her juices wet Mateo's lap. Afterwards, she dropped down on her knees and slipped his piece into her mouth, sucking its tip while stroking its shaft in her hand. Toni worked her lips and tongue on the dick so amazingly that Mateo exploded in her mouth. She then kissed him and exchanged the semen she had swallowed into Mateo's mouth and he swallowed.

Afterwards, the couple got themselves decent. Toni purchased the lingerie sets before they departed the boutique, as if they didn't just have fitting-room-sex.

***

Gangsta pulled to the curb before Ashley's crib. His G-Wagon made the first tracks in the new snow. He had not spoken with Ash since storming out on her, upset with how she came at him about Jade. And Gangsta just wanted her and Ash to gain some understanding that he was feeling Jade and she was having his baby, and nothing would change that. But if he knew what Ash knew, then he might have a change of heart.

He slogged through the snow to her front door. The temperature had dived so low that it was too damn child to breathe comfortably. Rolling clouds skittered over the black sky, threatening snow before morning.

Using the key Chase had given him, Gangsta entered the house and closed the door behind himself. The place was quiet and most of the lights were out. "Nobody's home," he considered. Gangsta decided he'd use the bathroom before leaving, and as he turned, he suddenly found himself at gunpoint with Major behind the trigger.

"Thought you'd be at the studio," Gangsta commented, not the least bothered by the gun.

Major lowered the gun and replied, "Takin' the night off to spend time wit' Ash." He clicked on a lamp.

"Maybe you should spend more time wit' Ash than at the studio," he told Major. "Where's she at, by the way?"

"Stepped out wit' Ty and the twins to grab a bite to eat." Major set his pole on the end table. "Don't you know how to knock before enterin'? I didn't know who the hell you were. Damn near got yo'self popped."

"Why knock?" Gangsta held up his keys. "Besides, you the last nigga I expect to pop somethin'," he added with a snort.

"Don't tempt me," Major warned. "Jus' ask yo' li'l flunky Playboy. He knows Major has no problem wit' poppin' pistols."

"Unlike you, PB's out puttin' in work in the streets. Probably out takin' over more of Diamond's turf."

"Admit it, Diamond scares you, doesn't he? And when he's back in the streets, then you'll have to face him," Major stated, watching Gangsta's face to measure the impact of his words.

Gangsta scoffed. "Diamond ain't shit. Can't wait to look him in the face before I down his ass. Major, only reason I haven't downed you personally thus far is on the strength of Ashley."

"Can't say the same about you," responded Major.

Gangsta continued, "As much as I hate to admit it, Ash loves you, fa real. And I'm sure since she feels that way about you, then you must be a real nigga. I may not like you, but I can respect a nigga who's real."

"Then I guess that's somethin' we have in common, Gangsta."

"Look, tell Ash I stopped by." Gangsta turned for the door and as a last second thought, he said, "Watch yo' back for Playboy."

***

"We have a problem."

"What is it?"

"More like who," Lynch corrected Tate.

They were seated in Lynch's Durango, parked in a vacant lot. Lynch had the headlights switched off, but not the engine. It was cold as hell outside and his heater was struggling to stay alive.

He continued, "It's Diamond. He threatened to tell Frank what he knows about me trying to have Frank offed if I refuse to help him get outta jail. And if Diamond does so, then you can bet your ass that Frank will come for me." Concern could be detected in his tone.

Tate blew into his hands to try keep warm. "Then we need to make a move before Diamond does. Have you set up anything wit' Frank Balistrieri yet?"

"Frank doesn't take any orders from me. So if I just call demanding he meet me in some back alley location, then he'll become suspicious. And believe me, if he suspects anyone of tryin' to double cross him they are likely to end up dead." Lynch exhaled sharply, then continued, "I'll try to come up with a way to make an easy target outta Frank. You just be sure Banks has his big guns available."

"Not a problem. Just provide the time and place," Tate assured him.

"As for Diamond, I have an idea how I'll deal with the son of a bitch," was all Lynch offered.

***

Ashley observed Tywanna drain her third glass of Kim Crawford wine. They were at Ash's crib in the kitchen, seated at the island having drinks. Ash knew her bestie was going through a lot. She'd never seen Ty so miserable before. As much as Ash tried to understand, she just wanted Ty happy again. Once Ty went to refill her glass, Ash grabbed the bottle from Ty, believing she'd already had more than enough to drink.

"Ty, since when did you become a drunk?" Ash asked, wanting Ty to get a grip on herself.

"Since I lost every damn thing, Ash!" Ty fumed. "I lost my home, my car, my baby...I even feel like I lost Diamond." Tears sheened her eyes. "I just need one more drink."

"No you don't," Ash told her, pulling the bottle further away as Ty reached for it.

"Fine, Ash, keep the damn bottle," Ty said with attitude. She dug inside her Vera Wang handbag sitting atop the island, came out with the pill bottle, and shook a tablet of Vicodin into her palm. "Can I at least have at least a glass of water to take my pills with?" The pharmacy label specified that the medication should be taken with food. She hadn't eaten dinner, and she still had no appetite.

Ashley noted it would be the second pill Tywanna would be taking in the hour. She was concerned about Ty using pity to abuse substances. Making her way over to the cabinet, Ash grabbed a glass, filled it partially with cold tap water, and then handed it to Ty, who washed down the pill. At least, unlike most painkillers, Vicodin left the mind clear.

"Ty," Ash began, "I know you also lost a lot of material things, but you can always get them back." She leaned a hip against the counter with her arms folded underneath her breasts. "Unfortunately, there's nothing you or Diamond or anyone can do to bring back Treasure."

Ty shook her head. "I hate that my mama saved me instead of my baby." Her voice broke.

"Uh-uh, girl. You shouldn't hate yourself. It's not your fault."

"Easy for you to say when you ain't the one who lost the baby. You have not one, but two beautiful kids that love you, Ash," Ty said almost bitterly.

Ashley threw her hands on her waist. "Don't sit there and make shit seem perfect because of my kids. I lost their farther, and that still hurts!" she said heatedly. Needing to calm herself, Ash took a deep breath. "Listen, girl," she began, looking Ty in the eye, all signs of her earlier hostility gone. "All I'm saying is, you ain't the only one who lost someone close. And the main person who shares the pain of your loss is Diamond."

Ty hung her head and quietly said, "I'm sure Diamond don't want me anymore. I can't even give him the family he wants." Tears crept down her face.

Ash wrapped an arm around Ty's shoulder in solace. "Diamond won't just stop loving you. Have you spoken with him about it?"

"I just couldn't tell him, Ash," she said through tears.

"It's best that you do, so you and him can figure things together. I'm sure he'll love you through this whole thing."

Ty raised teary eyes. "I just don't know how to deal with all of this."

Ashley pressed Ty's head to her chest in comfort. "I'm here for you, girl."

Major stepped into the kitchen, heading for the fridge. Immediately he realized he stumbled upon the girls having a moment. "Everything a'ight in here?" he asked out of concern. "Ty." He stepped near her. "I feel for you and Diamond. The two of you deserve to be happy together, and right now Diamond needs you".

"And I need him, too. It's hard on me without him, especially now."

"Maybe you should go see him. I'm sure he'd like to talk with you."

Ty shook her head. "I just don't wanna see Diamond in jail like that anymore. I want him home."

"Don't worry, Ty, he'll be home soon enough," Major assured her.

Ash piped in, "Major, will you gimme a moment alone with her?"

"You got it." He grabbed a bottled water from the fridge and then gave Ash a peck on the cheek before letting the girls be.

"Ty, girl." Ash took a seat on the stool. "I really don't like seeing you like this. Drinking and shit to try to cover your pain. You my girl, and I'll do all I can to help you get through this. But you gotta want my help."

"I love you like a sister, Ash. I don't know what I'd do without you," Ty told her sincerely.

"Girl, apparently you'd do some shit like cut your damn hair," Ash made light of the moment, pulling light laughter out of Ty.

"You don't like it?" Ty swiveled her head to display her new chic hairstyle. Her haircut favored the signature look of the singer Fantasia.

"No, it's cute. Brings out your features," Ashley complimented. Over the baby monitor, the twins were heard crying. "Girl, lemme go check on my babies." She went on her way.

While Ash was checking in on the twins, her iPhone began buzzing atop the island. Tywanna peeped at the phone's display and noticed the caller was Gangsta. Having a few choice words for his ass, she decided to answer the call herself.

"'Bout time you answered my damn call, Ash——"

"Uh-uh, rudeness," Ty interrupted. "This ain't Ashley."

"Tywanna?"

"Damn sure ain't Jade," she quipped.

Gangsta snorted. "You too, huh? Ash obviously told you about Jade being pregnant."

"Yup, sure did. And on the real, y'all don't deserve to have a baby. That's if she is really pregnant and you are really the daddy," she insinuated. "However, you and her deserve each other," she added distastefully.

"Dis about you losin' you and Diamond's baby? It's unfortunate that shit happened, but it's not me or Jade's fault, a'ight." His tone was stern.

Ty jumped to her feet and snapped. "Nigga, don't bring Diamond or our baby into this shit! You and Jade are good for each other since you both are some scheming-ass muthafuckas!"

"Fuck you talkin' 'bout?" Curiosity arose within him.

"For starters, I'm taking bout Lexi. Yeah, I know all about you killing her," she told him coldly.

"Does Ashley know?" he asked in a faint voice.

"Not yet, but she will once I——"

"I didn't mean for it to be Lexi who got killed," he said, cutting her short. "It was supposed to be Banks."

"And is that supposed to make it better?"

"Listen, Ty," he began solemnly, "I know Lex was y'all close friend so I understand the pain, because I felt the same way over Chase. And in between losing Lexi and Chase, don't you think Ash has been through enough pain? She doesn't need to know about this."

There was a stretch of silence. Tywanna took her seat and then exhaled deeply. "Alright, I won't tell her, at least not for now. I can't keep something like this away from her forever, so I'll give you the chance to tell her yourself, Gangsta."

"And when the moment is right, I will," he swore. "Forgive me or not, I didn't mean for it to be Lexi."

"Gangsta, forgiveness doesn't change the past." Tywanna ended the call.

Troublesome

Chapter 8

While Toni was seated in a booth taking a call, Mateo stood at the counter ordering their meals. They had stopped at McDonald's to grab a bite to eat. The two opted to make a walk-in order. Toni had some precautions about using drive-thru's. It made easy targets out of vehicles for lurking shooters, and she damn sure wasn't about to be caught slipping in the streets.

"Nigga talking 'bout he ain't got your paper right now, but he gonna pay you," one of Toni's goons reported. He had caught up with a nigga who ran off with some work Toni fronted him, and now the goon had the nigga's ass with a barrel to his dome. "Fuck you want me to do with his ass, Toni Montana?"

"Make that fuck nigga pay with his life," Toni ordered.

She heard the pistol crack three times in rapid succession before ending the call. Now that she was running her own outfit, Toni wasn't willing to allow no one to cross her without repercussion. Toni wanted to be known that she was the baddest bitch in the game.

Looking over the counter, Toni found Mateo still placing their orders. She noticed Gangsta enter the fast food joint with Playboy in tow. Once Gangsta took notice of her, then he made his way in her direction. The two hadn't seen each other in a while, although they'd been hearing each other in the streets. And from what they was hearing, each were out to put the streets under siege.

"I'm hearin' you got the streets puttin' some respect on yo' name, callin' you Toni Montana and shit." Gangsta smirked.

"And whoever don't respect it can say hello to my li'l friend," Toni replied, pulling the butt of her Glock from her Fendi handbag.

Gangsta chuckled. "Always knew you wasn't a bitch to be fucked wit'."

"Put yo' pole away, boo. This ain't that," Playboy piped in. "But I can use a bitch like you." He grinned.

"Li'l boy, you can't handle the type a bitch I am. What you need is a basic bitch," Toni told his ass.

"Damn, Playboy, she told you like it is," Gangsta cracked.

"Well, if you change yo' mind, then you can find me at my usual spot out at the Comfort suites. I'll show you jus' how much I can handle yo' ass," Playboy told her, sounding cocky. "I'm the man!"

Toni stood from the booth, then grabbed Playboy's genitals, causing him to buckle at the knees. "You may be a man, but I have the nuts." She set him free.

"Crazy bitch!" Playboy grunted, gingerly holding his balls.

"Like I told you before, you can't handle the type a bitch I am." Toni quirked an arched eyebrow.

"Yeah, whatever," Playboy steamed away.

Gangsta chuckled. "It's like that, Toni?"

"Straight like that."

"You always been the type a bitch wit' more nuts than most men - includin' Diamond. It was best for you to leave his ass and run yo' own crew."

"Gangsta, unlike you, I didn't suddenly decide to betray Diamond. He was the one that turned his back on me. And now I'm makin' a name for myself."

"I had my reasons, Toni. And even though I have a personal beef wit' Diamond, I never had hard feelings towards you," Gangsta explained.

"If it was up to me, then we'd all still be one crew. Chase wouldn't want us goin' against one another. It's like without him, we forgot the loyalty we once had. Now look at us - all out for the power over the same streets we once ran together," Toni expressed.

Gangsta had to admit Toni was right. "Part of me hates that shit is that way it is now between us. But whoever ain't wit' me in these streets is against me," he told her.

"Gangsta, then expect the streets to be rage and violence," Toni warned. She observed Mateo at the counter now collecting their order. "Just make you stay strapped in these streets. She left him with that thought as he watched her and Mateo exit the restaurant out into the falling snow.

Money, power, and respect have a way of turning friends into enemies.

***

"Yo, Racks, cut the beat."

For the fourth time in a row, Major messed up on a verse. Racks was working on a track. Major just couldn't seem to get focused in the booth tonight. What Gangsta had said about needing to spend more time with Ashley instead of in the studio was on his mental. But didn't Ash get that him chasing his dream meant it would consume a lot of his time and dedication? And things were beginning take off for him in the rap game.

Major started pushing "Money Shower" heavy. He and Rack's would be in the clubs tossing bands around to get the strippers and DJ's on board with the song. Before they knew it, V 100.7 had it on heavy radio rotation. Major's buzz in Milwaukee blew the roof off.

"Seem off tonight. Everything a'ight?" Racks said as Major stepped out from the booth.

Major flopped down on the sofa and said, "Jus' got some shit on my mind."

"Like what?"

"I'm startin' to second guess this rap shit," he breathed. "I'm dedicatin' so much of my fuckin' self to this shit. What if shit doesn't work out? Maybe I should give up this rap dream and jus' focus on the life I already have."

Racks shook his head. "Major, this rap shit is meant for you. There ain't many niggas wit' yo' skills. You been dreaming of being a rap star since we were li'l niggas, and now you have that opportunity. Take my word, soon you'll have major record labels lining up to sign you to a deal. It ain't about the money or fame; it's about the dream. But you gotta make a choice between the streets and music, Major."

Major understood where Racks was coming from. The two had been making music together since they were preteens, and Major planned to include Racks once his dreams came true. For a long time, Major dreamt that rap would be his way get out of the street life. And he knew his dream had a chance at becoming reality. But if he didn't choose to fully pursue his dream, then it could easily become a nightmare.

***

"You sure Major's in there?" Big Man questioned Ice.

"Yeah, I'm sure," Ice replied, annoyed. "The nigga posted on the Gram that he was in the studio working on new music."

"Ain't gon' lie, his track 'Money Shower' is a hit," Big Man admitted.

Ice shook his head. They sat in Big Man's Escalade, parked down the street from Major's studio. Ice was looking forward to burning Major's ass. It would be a win-win because not only would he be getting rid of his arch enemy but also a major competitor in the game. This was all part of Banks's plan to take over the streets. And killing Major would be a statement.

"There his ass is now," Big Man announced as Major followed by Racks emerged from the building. Ice gripped his Glock equipped with a thirty-shot clip.

"Pull up on the pussy nigga," he directed eagerly.

Major and Racks's breaths made white puffs of vapor as they stood before the studio saying their parting words. Big Man crept the Escalade down the street with its lights off. Once close enough, then Ice extended his arms out the window, aiming for Major with his Glock.

Boc, boc, boc, boc, boc!

Gunfire sprayed randomly around Major, mostly over his head. Instinctively, he dove onto the snow-sheathed sidewalk and rolled behind a parked car out of the way, barely escaping being shot. He drew his own weapon. Ice shot up the opposite side of the car, bullets shredding the metal, shattering the windows. Once the shots halted, then Major aimed over the car's hood and opened up on the Escalade as it sped away down the street.

Major was breathing hard. Mist plumed from his open mouth. "Racks?" he called out. Major turned and found Racks crumpled on the snow-covered sidewalk. There was a small halo of blood around his head.

A mixture of anger and pain instantly filled Major's heart. He reflected on Racks telling him he had to choose between music and the streets.

***

Snow started to fall like a thin white veil as Banks pulled into a parking spot at the strip mall. The reflection of his Aston Martin DB9 was in the window of the small cell phone establishment he parked before, which is where he'd usually go to pay his monthly cell bill.

The nail shop next door always reminded him of Lexi, being she used to frequent it for mani-pedi sessions. And today was no different. He sat in silence, thoughts and feelings of just how much he missed Lexi and loved her filling him. He thought about how beautiful she was the last night they were together, the very last night he'd see her alive and smiling before the gunfire. Then images of the light in her eyes fading away while he held her in his arms crept into his mind. He blinked away the saddening image and his eyes shone with tears. Damn, it deeply pained him that Lexi was dead and gone.

Banks took a moment to gather himself. He used the back of his hand to wipe away the tears. Looking himself in the eye in the rear-view mirror, he took a deep breath. He then grabbed the .40 Glock from his lap and tucked it on his waist before stepping out into the cold weather.

As he made his way towards the cell phone shop, he had his face buried in his iPhone, checking a text he'd just received. While distracted, he accidentally bumped into someone in passing.

"My bad," Ty grunted and continued on her way. She'd just exited the nail shop and was headed for her rental vehicle before bumping into Banks.

"I don't have anything against you, Ty," he called behind her. He added, "It's Diamond who I have something against." His breath frosted the air.

Stopping in her tracks, Ty turned, facing Banks, hand on her Dior bag, finding comfort knowing the .380 Diamond had given to her for her own personal security was packed inside. "The way I see it, if you have anything against Diamond, then you also have something against me, 'cause he and I are part of each other," she told him.

"Believe it or not, I respect Diamond. I can understand why you're down for him, jus' like Lexi was down for me. He and I had made a treaty that we wouldn't involve our girls in our beef. That was on the very night Lexi was...was killed." He spoke the final words in a quiet voice.

In that moment, Tywanna felt his sincerity. "I'm sorry about Lex. She was one of my besties, so losin' her is still hard on me too," she expressed. Her breath plumed into the cold air.

"And Lex genuinely cared about you a lot. Right before she was killed, she made me promise her that no matter what's between me and Diamond, I wouldn't harm you on the strength of your pregnancy."

"I never knew Lexi did that for me," Ty responded, speaking softly. Losing the baby hurt Ty even more now knowing that Lex tried to protect the baby. She looked away, but he saw tears in her eyes.

"Look, I didn't mean to mean to make you cry," Banks said gingerly.

"No, it's not you. It's just I...I lost me and Diamond's baby," she informed him.

Banks wasn't able to tell that Tywanna was no longer pregnant, being that the Dolce & Gabbana coat covered her up.

"I know the pain of losing an unborn child due to Lexi having a miscarriage," he said.

Ty looked at him, puzzled. "Lexi never talked with me about it. I didn't even know."

"It was a soft spot for her, that's why. And for me too. However, I'm sure you and Diamond will find a way to get through it together, like me and Lexi."

Now Ty was eyeing him sharply. "Banks, don't stand here actin' all like you're the best thing to happen to Lex, when you know it's disrespectful to her for you to be messin' with Jade," she told his ass.

"Jade and I are done," he replied with a scoff.

"It's a little too late for that Banks." Ty turned and walked back to her car. She fished out her pill bottle from the Dior bag and then took two Vicodin tablets. As of lately, she'd been using the medication to ease more than the pain. She bumped away the tears before starting the vehicle and driving on her way.

***

Jade had scheduled her appointment with the OB/GYN. She was in the doctor's room in the back of the clinic, and after a routine checkup consisting of a series of medical questions followed by blood and urine samples, she awaited her results. It had been some weeks since she'd taken the home pregnancy test, and Jade wanted to be sure all was well.

Jade couldn't help but wonder who was actually the baby's daddy. Though she let Gangsta believe it could be his, she wanted it to be Banks's. Jade knew Tywanna and Ashley thought ill of her being pregnant and she didn't give a fuck about them. They were always throwing Lexi in her face. All Jade cared about was Jade.

The gynecologist returned to the room, closing the door behind herself. Paying Jade little mind, the gynecologist read over the chart, revealing the results of Jade's tests. Finally the OB/GYN looked to Jade. "Ms. Matthews, I'll get right down to it. According to the lab test results, it turns out that you're not pregnant."

Jade couldn't believe what the OB/GYN had just told her. "No, that must be a mistake. I took a home pregnancy test and it showed positive," Jade said, sounding distraught.

"Sorry, Ms. Matthews, there's no mistake. Lots of those home pregnancy tests are inaccurate, which is why it's always best to come see a gyno," the OB/GYN responded.

"But what about me missin' my period? I haven't had it in weeks."

"Well, women can miss a menstrual cycle due to a number of reasons, stress being most common. And based on your high blood pressure levels from the lab test results, it appears stress would explain it," the OB/GYN explained.

"But I have to be pregnant. I just have to be," Jade said desperately.

The gyno placed a hand on Jade's knee in solace. "I know this is difficult for you. But I'm sure you will be happy to keep trying," she said gingerly. The gyno exited the room.

This can't be, Jade mused, distraught. She didn't know what the hell she was gonna tell Gangsta and Banks. They'd assume she'd been lying about being pregnant, and the fact that they were expecting a child is what kept both men from possibly killing her ass. Maybe she shouldn't tell them, and in the meantime she'd try to get pregnant by Gangsta or Banks before either of them knew the truth.

Jade failed to realize that if she lived her truth, then no one could use it against her.

Chapter 9

Playboy's breath made white puffs of vapor as he made his way from his duplex home to his Monte Carlo parked at the curb. He took a pull of his Newport, its cherry glowing red in the night. Snow crunched beneath his feet as he stepped up to his whip. He took one last pull on the cigarette before flicking away its butt into the snow-blanketed street.

As Playboy grabbed for the driver's door, a white Jeep Wrangler with darkened windows yielded to a halt beside him. Once he went for pistol on his waist, the Jeep's front passenger window dashed down and then came the muzzle of a AK-47. Playboy froze with his hand on the butt of his pistol. He was sure he was good as dead. Once the rear passenger window dashed down, he noticed it was Yul.

"Me don't dink it'll be a good idea to try it, boi. Less you wan' me brethren to blowtorch you bun," Yul warned.

"Hell's this about?" Playboy wanted to know, keeping his hand on the butt of his pistol.

"Me wan' discuss bidness wid you."

"Yeah, well, whatever it's about I'm sure you won't take no for an answer," Playboy commented.

Yul grinned. "Smart." He pushed open the door. "Come, now."

Reluctantly, Playboy climbed into the rear seat of the Jeep beside the Mega Don. Rasheym pulled off and Siah watched Playboy closely through the rearview mirror, AK-47 across his lap. Playboy was admittedly interested in knowing what business Yul had with him.

"So what's the business?" Playboy cut to the chase.

"Me wan' you to take over Gangsta's operation," Yul told him.

Playboy looked at him. "And why would I even consider that, comin' from you?"

"You don't stand to make it wid Gangsta widout me supply. But you, young one, can take over da operations an' wid me supplying you, you can make mo' money, dan you ever could wid Gangsta."

Playboy never wanted to pull the plug on Yul to begin with. It was Gangsta who was concerned about Yul's product being too risky for business since it was cut with fentanyl because if the cut is wrong, then fiends' hearts stop instantly from overdose. But Playboy didn't give a fuck about that. He only cared about how much money that shit produced. He didn't know if he had it him to betray Gangsta, and not out of fear, but instead respect.

"Let's say I'm willin' to be down wit' you. What about Diamond and his connect wit' the fuckin' goop Balistrieri? Gangsta says as long as they exist, then no one else stand a chance at controllin' the drug game in this city. Not even you," Playboy expounded.

Yul chuckled inwardly. "Gangsta don't know what me capable of. He seems to be de one who doesn't wan' murder Diamond. But no worries, mon, me an' me posse will put an end to Diamond an' his connect. Den us can rule de streets."

"There's one problem: Gangsta. Only way I'll be able to take over his operation is over his dead body," Playboy told him.

"Den you know what must be done," Yul stated.

Playboy understood.

After spinning around the block, Rasheym pulled to a stop beside Playboy's whip. Siah stepped out and pulled the door for Playboy, the AK-47 hanging from Siah's neck by its shoulder strap.

"Me expect you to come see me after you dead Gangsta. Or else," Yul posed sharply, eyeing Playboy.

With no further words, Playboy departed the Jeep, and then the Rastas dispelled.

Playboy didn't know if he was willing to betray Gangsta.

***

With dry-cleaning in hand, Toni emerged from the cleaners. She headed to her Benz where she placed the dry cleaning bag neatly inside the trunk. As she made her way for the driver's door her iPhone buzzed, and she fished it out of Bottega Veneta shoulder bag. Checking the phone's display, Toni saw it was a blocked call.

"You're callin' me blocked so we shouldn't be talkin'," Toni answered with no clue who the caller was.

"Or maybe it's best we talk," the caller replied. It was Lynch.

Toni paused, hand on the door handle. "Hell did you get my number, Lynch?" she questioned, frustration in her tone.

"Let's just say I have my ways," he answered smugly. "Now I expect you to meet me in Red Arrow Park in twenty." Click.

"Ugh!" Toni grimaced and crashed the phone into the street, then stomped on it with her Jimmy Choo stiletto boots. She wasn't willing to take a chance of Lynch having her phone line wire tapped.

Toni knew meeting with Lynch wasn't a good idea. She wanted nothing to do with the Fed. He wasn't to be trusted. But she understood the only way to get Lynch off her case was to meet with him once and for all.

Toni jumped in her Benz. She pressed the "push to start button" and then zipped down the snow-cleared street.

Red Arrow Park was located in Central downtown. The park was flanked by businesses, big and small. Most days the park was lively, and today was no different. For once the weatherman was right. The snow had stopped in the middle of the night and now the sun shone brightly, warming both land and people.

Toni made her way through the park until she spotted Lynch seated on a bench alone near the ice rinks. He was drinking from a cup of Starbucks coffee, and there was a half-folded newspaper across his lap. Toni casually took a seat on the far end of the bench, setting her bag beside her and crossing her legs. She observed the less than pleasant man while he looked off in the distance at the snow-covered scene.

"Something told me you'd come," Lynch said evenly.

"Why'd you call me here?" Toni asked gruffly, cutting to the chase.

Lynch set the cup of joe on the ground beside his feet and then fixed Toni with his frigid blue eyes. "I need you to testify against Diamond," he told her.

"Shoulda known this would be about Diamond," she huffed. "And why would I testify against him?"

"Because, goddammit, had it not been for me raiding the stash house and sparing you when Diamond had a gun to your head, then he would have killed your ass!" Lynch raved

Toni held his glare. "I'd rather kill or be killed than snitch, unlike Pelle. And to prove it, I'm the one who killed Pelle's snitch-ass," she told him.

Lynch never suspected she was the one who murdered Pelle. He figured Diamond had sent the hit. It pissed Lynch off to know Toni was the reason that his star witness wasn't able to testify against Diamond and put the son of a bitch away for good. Right then he regretted sparing Toni from being killed by Diamond.

"I shoulda known it was you. Where do you get off thinkin' you can take the law in your own hands?" Lynch breathed coldly.

Toni stood, grabbed her bag, and hung it off her shoulder. "Justice and the law are separate issues," she replied obstinately.

Toni turned as though to leave, and Lynch came up from underneath the newspaper across his lap with his firearm. In a motion almost too fast to follow, Toni reached inside her bag, gripping her Glocks, and squeezed the trigger.

Blocka, blocka, blocka!

Boom, boom, boom, boom!

The two exchanged shots, and bystanders either hit the ground or took cover behind whatever they could. Lynch assumed he had Toni dead, but she peeped his holster without its weapon immediately. Toni never pulled the Glock out of her bag, bustin' shots through it at Lynch until he scuttled backwards in retreat. Once far enough away from the trigger-happy bitch, Lynch quickly turned on his heels and sprinted away with bullets whizzing by him.

Toni turned and fled towards her Benz. She tossed the ruined bag into the passenger seat as she jumped inside the whip. Speeding away, she heard sirens in the distance. Out of frustration, she hit her clenched fist down on the steering wheel.

She couldn't believe Lynch had the audacity to approach her with testifying against Diamond. Toni just hoped that once Diamond returned to the streets there wouldn't be any smoke between them. *I'd hate to have to kill Diamond*, she mused, *but I will.*

***

"I spoke wit' Levin. He told me he met wit' Lynch," Major told Diamond. They were on a collect call.

"And?" Diamond urged.

"And Levin says judgin' by the look on Lynch's face when he mentioned Balistrieri, he's sure Lynch will be to see the D.A, if he hasn't already. Now all there is to do is wait."

"I've already been waiting too damn long," Diamond replied, aggravated. "Listen, if I'm not back in the streets in a week tops, and then I want you to go see Balistrieri. I'm sure he'll be able to convince the pig to get me outta here one way or another."

"Will do." Major understood what Diamond wanted him to do. "How you holdin' up in there?" he wanted to know.

Diamond snorted. "Hate it in here. Food's garbage, guards are hard cases, and most niggas are willin' to rat you out or take you out or both," he stressed. "But tough times don't last. Only tough niggas do."

"Facts," Major concurred.

"How 'bout you? I'm sure you holdin' shit down out there."

"In between takin' care of business and problems, shit ain't easy out here. Not to mention everyone's out to take over by any means - includin' Toni," Major told him.

"Yeah, word travels from the streets to jail fast. I'm hearin' she's makin' a name in the streets."

"I'll say! Niggas are even callin' her Toni Montana," Major huffed. "Had it not been for her ass, you wouldn't even be on lock, and she had the audacity to tell me you owe her one, for Pelle."

Diamond understood Toni killing Pelle prevented Pelle from being able to testify in court against him. But Diamond couldn't overlook the fact that Toni had brought Pelle into the crew, so she was responsible for taking him out.

"Pelle got what he had comin' so I owe Toni nothin'. And she, too, will get what she got comin'. So will the others," Diamond stated. "Major, I know it ain't easy holdin' shit down in the streets.

It takes a certain type a nigga to do so. Maybe you're ready to take over."

"Been thinkin', Diamond. It's not for me," Major told him.

"And why not?" he asked, puzzled. Diamond was sure that Major would jump at the chance to take over the operation.

"I'd rather focus on pursuing my rap dreams," he replied evenly. Major had chosen to get out of the street life after Racks's murder. Racks had been right about things picking up for him in the rap industry and he wanted to seize the opportunity.

"Diamond," Major went on, "I got mainstream record labels lookin' to sign me to a rap deal. But if I continue to live what I rap, then more than likely I won't live long enough to make it out the streets. 'Cause we both know the outcome is either a cell or a casket. And I want more than that."

"And I wanna see you make it out the streets, Major. I believe you should pursue yo' rap dreams. All I ask is jus' hold shit down until I return to the streets," Diamond said.

"And when you do return, then what about you, Diamond? We both know the streets will claim you one way or another eventually," Major stressed.

"You don't have to be concerned about me, Major."

"It's Tywanna I'm more so concerned about," he interrupted. "And so should you be. Ty needs you, Diamond. She's goin' through it since losin' the baby." Major spoke the final words gingerly.

There was a stretch of silence between them. Diamond finally found his voice to speak. "Listen, I do understand what Ty's goin' through. She's the main reason why I need to get outta here, because I know I should be there for her," he expressed. "And believe me, Major, I want more outta life than the street life that I know. And once I'm finally outta the street life, then I know I can have it."

The automatic voice chimed in warning there was one minute remaining on the call.

"Major, jus' hold shit down until I return to the streets," Diamond told him.

Major knew that Diamond was anxious to get back to the streets. He just hoped that when Diamond did, then he'd be prepared for the beef, bullets, and blood awaiting him.

***

The waitress handed the two women each a menu before waltzing away. Sandra, Tywanna, and Ashley occupied a table in the Cheesecake Factory.

"I still don't understand why you practically dragged my ass here to see her," Ty said to Ash, referring to San. She was still upset with her mother, and had Ash told her she would be at the eatery, then Ty would not have come.

"Ty, we need to talk with you," Ash said with concern in her tone.

Ty's arched eyebrows furrowed. "Talk with me about what?"

"About your drug and alcohol problem, Ty."

"Problem? I don't have a damn problem," she replied, sounding offended.

Sandra sighed deeply. "Sweetie, we get that you are going through a hard time since losing the baby. Although it's no reason for you to be drinking heavily and abusing painkillers just to cover your feelings," she stressed.

Over the weeks, Ashley and Sandra noticed Tywanna relying more and more on alcohol and Vicodin. Obviously it was her way of coping with the pain, guilt, and shame she felt after losing her baby, but Ty didn't believe she had a problem.

"For the record, I'm grown so I can drink. And the pills are for my damn head," Ty said defensively.

"Ty." Ash reached over the table and grabbed her hand, "You've been usin' both more than you should, and it's gettin' outta control. Maybe you need to go to rehab."

"No." She backed up and snatched her hand back. "I'm fine, okay?"

"Sweetie, abusing will only cover the pain it won't change a thing. I know that you're hurt," Sandra said, speaking gingerly.

"You don't know because you're not the one who's goin' through what I am." Ty's voice broke as pain filled her eyes. "It's your damn fault any of this happened," she snapped.

In that moment, Sandra knew she needed to tell Ty the truth about what happened to her dad. "Tywanna, listen——"

"No, you listen!" Ty cut her short. "I hate that you decided to save me over my baby. And now I may never be able to give Diamond a child. Neither of you know what I'm goin' through!" she shouted.

"We're just tryin' to help you, Ty," Ash said pleadingly.

Ty shot to her feet and spat, "Well, there's nothin' you can do to help, except leave me the hell alone!" She steamed away for the exit.

"Ty, wait!" Ash started after her until San grabbed Ash by the arm, stopping her.

"Let her go," San told her. "She's right. Only person who will be able to help her is Diamond."

Chapter 10

Diamond stepped out of the county jail a free man. After a few months of lockdown, he was finally back in the streets. And he was out to get even.

Making his way through the light snowfall, Diamond headed for Levin's BMW idling at the curb. Levin was the only one aware of Diamond's release. Once Diamond stepped into the passenger seat, Levin pulled off.

"Took you long enough to get me outta that hellhole," Diamond commented.

"Apparently Agent Lynch took a few days before finely finally going to see the D.A.," Levin responded.

Diamond scoffed, "Lynch has another thing comin' if he thinks I'll let him get away wit' double-crossin' me. Two can play that game."

"I'm sure," Levin said.

"What about all of my bank accounts that were frozen and possessions that were seized by the fuckin' Feds?" Diamond wanted to know.

Levin steered the BMW onto the highway. "Actually, after the conspiracy charges against dismissed, I was able to have everything taken care of. Your bank accounts have been unfrozen and all possessions relinquished. I just advise you to sweep your places and vehicles for bugs." He smirked at Diamond.

"Levin, I'ont know how to repay you for all you've done."

"How about you just pay me double my retainer fee like you offered and consider us even?" the attorney half-joked.

Diamond chuckled. "Done."

The windshield wipers brushed away the light snowfall. The snow sifted out of the black sky and made pale, shifting patterns on the dark streets.

"Now that you're out, I'm sure you can't wait to see Tywanna," Levin commented. He knew how the couple felt about each other.

"I jus' hope she'll be happy to see me," Diamond replied in a low voice, looking out the passenger window at the snow blanketed scene. He still hadn't spoken with Ty since the day she bailed out during the visit.

"And why wouldn't she be, Diamond?"

"Because I know she puts a lot of the hurt on me for the loss of our child, since I wasn't able to be there for them. Jus' wish there was some way I can make it up to her. "

"Unfortunately, Diamond, you can't make up for lost time. All you can do is give her as much of your time as you can."

Diamond looked to Levin. "Once I finish up my business in the streets, I'm out. Then I'll be able to focus all my time on me and Ty bein' together and us havin' a family."

"Maybe that's what's best for you both."

The BMW slowed as they left the highway and cruised to the intersection of 7th and North Street. As they went for a right turn, a semi-truck blindsided, them T-boning the BMW. Upon impact of the collision, the BMW's airbags deployed and its driver's side was crushed inward. The collision left Levin badly injured with broken bones and a bloodied head, while Diamond had only been disoriented. Once Diamond shook off the daze, he immediately checked on Levin, who was unconscious. Diamond looked over and observed the driver hop out of the truck. It was Lynch! Diamond saw him raise a gun. It glinted in the light from the street lamp. He ducked in his seat, out of the line of fire.

Boc, boc, boc, boc, boc!

Bullets shattered some windows and deflated the airbags. Unfortunately, Levin had took two deadly shots to the chest. Diamond couldn't take his eyes off the shadow moving steadily toward the vehicle. If Diamond didn't do something fast, then Lynch would dead him too.

Leaning over Levin's corpse, Diamond shoved open the driver's door and then pushed the body out of the BMW onto the snow-sheeted street. He then hurriedly slid behind the steering wheel. Lynch fired rapidly at the BMW as it hastily fish-tailed away. Diamond kept his head low as Lynch continued to fire a succession of shots behind the BMW. At the nearest corner, Diamond made a wide turn in order to avoid more shots.

"Dammit," Diamond curse under his breath out of frustration and slammed a clenched fist down on the steering wheel. He was sure Lynch wouldn't just let him out of jail without eventually coming for him. Now Diamond knew he had to do something about Lynch before Lynch could make any more moves on either him or Frank Balistrieri.

Diamond discarded the wrecked BMW some blocks later and began traveling on foot. Luckily he'd been brought a change of attire appropriate for the winter weather because the temperature was hovering above freezing. Figuring it wouldn't be such a good idea for him to go directly home, Diamond headed towards Ashley's place. He climbed the front porch steps and went directly to the door. He rapped on the tinder door. A moment later, the door was pulled open.

Major wasn't expecting to find Diamond in the doorstep. He stepped aside and let Diamond into the warmth, closing the door behind him.

"Obviously Lynch followed through on his end," Major said. He and Diamond stood in the front room.

"Yeah, and apparently that muthafucka only got me outta jail in order to try to body my ass," Diamond fumed.

"I take it he came after you tonight," Major assumed.

"Yeah, he did. Lynch is willin' to do any fuckin' thing jus' to prevent me from tellin' what I know about him to Balistrieri," Diamond scoffed. "He killed Levin."

"What you gon' do about Lynch now?" Major wanted to know.

"Only thing for me to do is body Lynch's ass," Diamond stated. He know it was either him or Lynch.

"And what about Balistrieri? Are you gonna tell him about Lynch?"

"It's best that I do."

"Agreed," Major replied. He noticed blood stains on Diamond's hand and imagined it must have come from Levin. "Might wanna go clean yo'self up."

Diamond then noticed the blood himself. It got on his hand when pushed Levin's body out the car. He went to the bathroom and washed his hands before returning to the front room.

"Look, how 'bout you gimme a ride?" Diamond said.

While Diamond waited, Major stepped into the bedroom to grab his keys. In that moment, the front door opened and Ash and the twins entered. Seeing their uncle Diamond, the twins scurried to him and Diamond squatted and enveloped them both into his embrace. Afterwards, Ash removed the twins' coats and sent them into the dining room with the box of Little Caesar's pizza she had brought with her.

"Good to see you finally out, Diamond," Ash said as she shrugged out of her own coat and hung it on the rack with the twins'. "Does Ty know you're out yet?"

"No. I was hopin' to find her here wit' you."

"Actually, Ty hasn't seemed to want to be in my company lately." She sighed.

"What do you mean?" he asked curiously.

"I mean, she hasn't been much of herself ever since losin' the baby," Ash told him in a low voice. "I'm worried about her, Diamond."

"Don't worry, Ash, I'm here for her now."

"She really needs you," Ash said sympathetically. "And I'm sure she'll be happy to see you after so long. You'll be able to find her at the Marriott."

"The Marriott? Why's Ty there? She's supposed to be stayin' at her mama's place," he commented.

"She's upset with San right now," Ash let him know. She put a hand on his arm and said, "Diamond, make sure you be there for Tywanna."

Diamond heard the concern in her voice. "I will be," he pledged.

With his keys in hand, Major returned to the front room. He gave Ashley a peck on her lips. Ash then headed into the dining room where the twins were, leaving Major and Diamond be.

"Part of me has to get used to you and Ash bein' together," Diamond admitted.

"I'm sure, bein' that she was wit' Chase for so long," Major mentioned. "It bothers Gangsta that I'm wit' her," he breathed, shaking his head

"Trust me, he doesn't want Ash wit' anyone beside Chase," Diamond told him, knowing how close Gangsta had been to Chase.

"Yeah, he made that clear to me. Look, shit's unfortunate how things came to an end for Ash and Chase. However, I'm wit' Ash now. And a nigga loves her ass, Diamond," Major expressed.

"Major, you a good nigga, and since Ash is wit' you, then you must make her as happy as Chase did. Jus' know that I believe you and Ash are right for each other. "

"Good to know," Major replied gratefully. "Here, jus' take my whip for now." He handed Diamond the keys to his Audi. "And jus' in case, there's a stick in the stash."

"Fa sho'." Diamond dapped Major before bouncing.

***

Pulling up to Frank's mansion, Diamond pressed the intercom system on the security gate and announced himself then waited patiently for admission. Moments later, the iron gates swung open. Riding down the long, winding driveway, Diamond was greeted by Little and Alphonse. Once Diamond debarked from the Audi, the two escorted him inside and then to den to see the mob boss, Frank Balistrieri.

"Why don't you have a seat, Diamond?" Frank offered. He was seated on the antique chaise lounge, sporting a silk Givenchy robe, pajamas, and loafers, a plume of smoke curling up into the still air from the Cuban cigar between his fingers. Across from him, Diamond sat on the matching antique sofa.

Frank stuck the stogie in his mouth and talked around it. "Good to see you finally outta the can. Believe me, I know what it's like. Was found guilty of the charges of blackmail and illegal gambling and was sentenced to ten years in federal prison. I was released after serving six. That was long ago, and the fuckin' Feds still have it out for me." He shook his head. "Luckily, Agent Lynch was able to get you out."

"Mr. Balistrieri," Diamond began slowly, "that's actually what I'm here about." He could read that he had Frank's attention.

Frank took the stogie from his mouth and tapped a big chunk of ash in the tray on the coffee table. "Go on; humor me."

Diamond sat hunched, forearms on his knees, eyeing Frank. "Lynch can't be trusted. He's who put me on lockdown, and the only reason he even got me out is because I threatened to tell you everything I know about him. And tonight he tried to off me jus' to shut me up for good."

"And what is it you could possibly know about Agent Lynch that I he'd wanna off you over?" Frank inquired.

"Lynch has been out to betray you. Some time back he even came at me wit' an under-the-table offer that I turned down. And he also planted a rat among my crew in an attempt to indict me jus' to use my freedom as a bargainin' chip if I roll over on you. He's the one who sent the hit the night you and I were together. Think about it: he's the only other person who knew where to locate us. Lynch wants you gone and anyone who's loyal to you."

Now Frank sat straight up on the chaise. "And why didn't you tell me any of this before, Diamond?" he pressed.

"Mr. Balistrieri, pardon me for not tellin' you before now," Diamond reasoned.

"That son of a bitch," Frank hissed under his breath. He rose to his feet and began to pace, thoughts of all he was just told churning around in his head. "I shoulda seen it coming. Agent Lynch needs me out of the way so I can no longer hold the murders of a couple cops over his head. He wouldn't have to answer to anyone and could seize control of the drug trade. I must get rid of Agent Lynch immediately." He halted, looked at Diamond, then added, "And I'm handing you the honor of whackin' him."

Diamond nodded his understanding. "Mr. Balistrieri, you should know that once I tie up the loose ends, then I'm gettin' outta the game."

"Are you sure about that, Diamond? I need you runnin' things. Don't get me wrong here; I like Major. The kid has potential. But an operation is only as elite as the man who runs it. And there ain't many men like you," Frank declared.

"I'm flattered, Mr. Balistrieri, but it won't change my mind. And as for Major, let's not forget he's the one who found a way to clear my debt wit' you while runnin' things when I was in lockdown. But he's already made it clear to me that the game isn't what he wants any more than I do," Diamond expounded.

Frank took a deep drag of the stogie and blew out a big smoke cloud. "How about this: you continue to run the operation only until you find someone who is like you to take over," he bargained.

Diamond stood. "I'll do it. And I'll be sure to find someone who will be a good fit for the position," he pledged.

Frank bit down on the cigar and talked around it. "In this game good will get a man killed. The man has to be the best of the best. That's one of the keys to this. You will end up being a rare survivor in this deadly game, Diamond."

Following his rendezvous with Frank, Diamond was pushing the Audi through the snow-sheathed streets. His thoughts drifted in the air. He understood what it would take for him to get out of the game.

***

"Diamond," Tywanna murmured, unexpectedly finding him at the door of her hotel room.

Diamond held her with his eyes, immediately recognizing she'd cut her hair, was thinner than he was used to, and had bags beneath her brown eyes. Even still, he found her beauty.

"I'm here for you now," Diamond told her in a low voice

She dove into his arms and began to cry in relief. He enveloped her in a tight embrace and gingerly stroked the back of her head.

"And I'm not leavin' you ever again."

The couple stepped inside the room, Diamond closing the door behind them. Ty moved over to the love seat as Diamond shrugged out of his Moncler coat and tossed it over the arm of the sofa before joining her. He noticed on the coffee table there was a nearly-empty bottle of Ciroc and a pill bottle with only a few tablets of Vicodin remaining, and it reminded him of Ashley mentioning Ty bit being not much of herself lately. It troubled Diamond that because of pain and suffering, Ty seemed to be in a downward spiral. But now he was there to uplift her.

I missed you more than you could ever know, Ty," said Diamond.

"And Diamond, I missed you too," Ty replied in a small voice. "I'm sorry that I didn't come back to visit you, but I just couldn't stand to see you in jail anymore."

"Well, you don't have to worry about that anymore now that I'm home. Things can go back to normal."

Ty rose and stepped over to the nearest window, staring out at an eerie panorama of gigantic, snow swept buildings and fuzzy lights. "Diamond, don't think that you bein' home fixes every damn thing, because it doesn't. Maybe had you been here, then things would still be normal." She turned facing him with tear-filled eyes. "I been through a lot while you were gone."

"I know," he sympathized with her.

"There's a lot of things you don't know, Diamond." Frustrated, she continued, "For starters, I didn't have a home to live in or even my own car to get around. Then I was thrown in jail, and had it not been for Toni bein' there with me and protectin' me, it coulda been worse. Also there was the whole thing with the stripper. It wasn't so easy for me to get over the fact that you was with her. And the worst thing was the accident. Not only did I nearly lose my life, but I lost our baby. For me, Diamond, goin' through those things are more than you know." Tears streamed down her cheeks.

Diamond could see her pain and suffering. He rose and stepped up to her, gently placing his hands on each of her arms, then tranquilly said, "Ty, I can't apologize enough that you had to go through all of that. But you no longer have to worry about bein' wit'out a crib and whip or anything, 'cause I'm here to provide for you. You don't have to rely on anyone else to protect you, 'cause I'll protect you wit' my life. You don't have to worry about the idea of me bein' wit' another bitch behind yo' back, 'cause I'ont want nobody else but you. As for you grievin' over the loss of our baby, she'll always be a part of us. Together we can get through anything." He wiped away her tears.

Ty hung her head. "There's another thing you don't know," she muttered. Even though she feared Diamond wouldn't want her anymore, she just had to tell him. "Diamond, I——"

"Whatever it is can wait 'cause I've already wasted long enough," Diamond intervened. He lowered his mouth onto hers and kissed hungrily. It was obvious how badly he was thirsting for her love and affection.

Ty suddenly drew back. "Diamond wait," she said in close to a whisper. Even though she wanted him more than the air she breathed, she felt the need to tell him about the fact she might not be able to conceive. "I may not——"

"Shhh." Diamond proceeded with kissing her and she obliged with no more words.

Ty helped him out of his sweater and then went for his jeans. She took in how damn fine he was, admiring the paper thin scar that sliced through his right eyebrow, which exaggerated his thuggish manner. Once Diamond was naked, it was his turn to remove the short pink crop top that left Ty's brown midriff bare and the tight jeans she wore, leaving her ass naked. Her nipples were hard, and so was his dick.

Diamond lifted Tywanna and sat her on the window sill. She sucked his lower lip and guided his long, hard piece deep into her slippery twat, softly moaning as each inch of him filled her. While he thrust back and forth, she spread her legs wide open and held onto his shoulders. In between the cold weather outside and their body heat, the window became fogged with a film of moisture.

"Mmm, yes, Diamond. Yes, baby. I missed this dick so much," Ty moaned as he drilled her pussy. He was encouraged to bury his dick down to his balls inside her with each thrust.

"Damn, love, I missed how good you feel," he groaned. Her snatch gripped at his joint. He enjoyed the moist tightness of her walls embracing his tender dick.

Tywanna tossed her head back and raked her nails over his back as his throbbing, long dick hit her G-spot. She let out screams of passion and pleasure. Diamond was turned on knowing that he was pleasing his lover. He pulled himself out of her then lowered onto his knees and greedily sucked and licked her kitty, causing her to arch her back.

"Oooh, baby! Yo' lips feel so damn good on me!" Ty moaned loudly. She palmed Diamond's head and pressed his face deep between her legs, encouraging him to eat her out until she came.

Diamond used his fingers to spread her pussy lips in order to flick his warm tongue over her clit and suck it into his mouth. Eyes tightly shut, head tilted back and mouth agape, Ty moaned and trembled as she creamed into his mouth and some got on his beard. Diamond loved the taste of her.

Tywanna pushed his head away and then she turned around, planting her hands on the window sill, arching her back for Diamond's easy access to her wet-shot. "Fuck me good and hard," she purred, looking back at him over her shoulder.

Diamond stuff himself inside her snug hole. "Dis how you want me to fuck you?" Diamond grunted as he dug her out. Their flesh made a clapping sound with each stroke.

"Aaahh…yes, Diamond just like that, baby," she moaned. Her pussy was ready to explode!

Diamond used his hands to spread her ass cheeks, giving him more room to fuck Ty deeper from behind. And Ty took his big dick with pleasure. Their reflection showed in the window pane as snow fell lazily outside.

"Damn, Ty," Diamond groaned once he released a long nut deep inside her tightness. "It's been so long," he panted.

"Too long," Ty added. She wrapped her arms around his neck, raised on her tiptoes, and kissed him. "Diamond, I——" she started, thinking to tell him about the possibility of not being able to conceive. And then, after thinking now wasn't the right time, she said, "Love you."

"And I luh yo' ass too, Ty. Won't nothin' change that," Diamond promised. "Now let's pack yo' things and go home.

Troublesome

Chapter 11

"And what did Balistrieri have to say about Lynch?"

"Wants me to whack 'im."

Diamond and Major were in the theater, seated at the mini bar. Being there and seeing the excessive bullet holes visible in the walls reminded Diamond of the eventful night when Lynch raided the stash house.

Diamond took a swig from his glass of Henny. "And now I jus' gotta get at 'im when the opportunity presents itself. And whenever it does, I'ma put his ass in the dirt," he vowed.

"And what about the others? Once Gangsta and Banks find out you're back in the streets, then they'll definitely come after you too. And maybe even Toni," Major stressed.

"Then let 'em come." Diamond said those words defiantly, and Major noticed his eyes were as humbling as the muzzle of a pair of pistols.

"Enough said." Major took a drink from his own glass.

Diamond stood from the bar stool and began pacing with his drink in hand. "Major," he started tranquilly, "I want you to know that I appreciate you runnin' things while I was in lock down and findin' a way to take care of my debt wit' Balistrieri. And I respect that you remained loyal."

"I know you woulda done all the same for me, Diamond," Major replied weakly. He adjusted himself on the stool, then said, "What more do you have to prove in the streets? You already have money, power, and respect."

Diamond halted his pace. "It's not about any of those things for me anymore. I only have one more thing to prove: it's possible to make it out the streets wit'out endin' up in prison or dead. But I have business to finish in the streets before I can prove it. Diamond, I jus' want for you to see a future outside of the street life. That's why I chose to pursue my rap dreams, especially after Racks got killed due to beef over streets that are loyal to none," Major vented.

"I feel you, and I really want you to follow yo' dream and make a future for yo'self."

"And I have big dreams and a bright future, Diamond. I'm talkin' sellin' out world tours and havin' diamond records," he shared with a level of excitement

"And you have the talent and potential to make it happen." Diamond believed in him.

"I've even been in talks wit' Gucci Mane. Nigga wanna sign me to his record label, So Icey Entertainment. Even asked me to shoot out to the ATL so I can make some music wit' him at the Brick Factory studio. And I wanna take you wit' me, Diamond. As my manager. That way we can get out the streets together."

"Listen, Major, bein' in the rap game is yo' dream, not mine, so it's best that you pursue it yo'self. However, I'll support you all the way," Diamond told him.

"'Preciate it. And you know I'll always be down for you," Major assured him. "But I gotta know, what is yo' dream, Diamond?"

Diamond took a swig of Henny. "To live a normal life one of these days."

***

Big Man held the choppa leveled on Ice's chest. Ice pushed the weapon's barrel away and everyone around ducked out of the line of fire of the deadly weapon.

Big Man busted out laughing. "You scary-ass niggas, it ain't even loaded!"

"Shit ain't funny, Big Man. Don't point that mu'fucka at me again," Ice protested.

Big Man set the choppa in Ice's lap and cracked, "Dawg, yo' ass need that mu'fucka 'cause you can't shoot." Laughter circled the room. "You missed Major's ass twice already!"

"Bet I won't miss that bitch nigga again."

Banks piped in, "Ay, will you niggas quit playin' around and help bag up this work?"

In the back room of Magic Clippers, Banks and his top-level gang members were prepping product to be distributed to the trap spots. While Tate was in the front area of the shop cutting patron's hair his enforcer Dub, who was a light- skinned cat with a bald head, long braided goatee, and dark, beady eyes, watched over the drugs like a hawk. Even though Tate trusted Banks and his boys, Dub trusted none, with the exception of Tate, who he'd ride or die for.

Big Man packaged an ounce of the boy. "How much money do we stand to make off all of this work?" he asked, referring to the two kilos they were prepping to move.

"Nothin' compared to what we'll be makin' once we eventually off that Frank Balistrieri muthafucka," Banks replied. "Then we'll start havin' so many bricks that these two won't be about shit!"

"Sounds good and all, but know what happened when we pulled up on his ass the first time. He was in a fuckin' bulletproof whip! A muthafucka like that is untouchable," Ice said as he weighed some 'ron on the digital scale.

"Tate says the alphabet boy Lynch is workin' on it. But for now, we gon' focus on expandin' in the streets," Banks told him, placing packaged work in the duffle.

"Word is the nigga Diamond's out. That means now we gotta beef wit' him and Gangsta over the streets," Big Man stressed.

"And the bitch Toni Montana makin' noise in the streets, too," Ice mentioned. "Ain't no fuckin' way a bitch gonna take over while I'm around," he scoffed.

"I ain't lettin' none of 'em stop us from runnin' the streets. We gon' paint the streets red," Banks declared. He knew now that Diamond was back in the streets the beef would intensify. And shit with Gangsta was only a matter of time before it came to a head. Then there was that bitch Toni to add to the mix of problems.

Banks understood that the streets were under siege among the different gangs and there were bound to be a slew of gangland murders.

***

Junkies slogged through the snow, making their way to the apartment building operated by Gangsta, where they copped a fix. They were located in a not-quite-gentrified neighborhood of low-end apartments that left very few trees to soften the scene. Instead, there was lousy upkeep at the redbrick apartment building and piles of filthy snow packed back against the building.

Gangsta and Playboy's breaths made white puffs of vapor as they stood outside of the apartment building during the frigid evening. They were among a group of Gangsta's pack-boys who were makin' plays.

Playboy blew in his hands to try keep warm. "Fuck we doin' posted out here freezin' our asses off when you got these niggas for this shit?" he griped. The air was so cold it hurt his throat when breathing it in.

"Playboy, don't forget, at one point we used to be these same niggas here posted on the block wit' that pole cocked, ready to bang a nigga for his spot. So I'm posted out here to let niggas know ain't shit changed, in case a nigga thinkin' 'bout bangin' me for mine," Gangsta told him."

"More than anyone, it's Banks we need to be worried 'bout. See how that nigga come for you at the gamble spot?" Playboy materialized a Newport and lit it up.

Gangsta scoffed. "That pussy nigga has his chance and didn't take me out. Now it's my turn. Plus, now that Diamond's back in the streets, he may get to Banks before I do." Word had gotten to him about Diamond's release and Gangsta was eager to hit up Diamond just as much as he was Banks. "Banks and Diamond gon' feel my heat," he added bitterly.

"And how 'bout Toni Montana? That crazy-ass bitch and her gang out here in these streets puttin' in work. She already had a few of our boys murked over on Nash Street and set up shop. Her ass is becomin' a threat," Playboy stressed. He took a drag of the cigarette and blew out a big smoke cloud.

"Toni knows I ain't against bodyin' a bitch. I'll try getting' an understandin' wit her before it goes there. If not, then that's on her."

Gangsta observed the pack-boys moving work, knowing he was running short on supply.

"Gangsta, even after dealin' wit' all of them, then there still those Rastas," Playboy brought up. He'd decided against telling Gangsta about Yul's proposal because he wasn't sure of it.

Gangsta waved off the comment and stated, "Yul don't put fear in a nigga like me. He can get it too."

"Well, I'ont think it's such a good move to cut him off. I mean, he supplied us wit' as much work as we needed. Where we gon' find another plug like that, G?" Playboy tried to reason with Gangsta.

Gangsta eyed him. "Where's this shit comin' from all of a sudden?" he interrogated.

"Jus' forget I even brought it up." Playboy bowed out. He took one last drag of the Newport, then dropped the butt and ground it under his Timberland boot.

"Look, PB, I refuse to go grovelin' back to Yul. I'll find another plug, a'ight?" Gangsta told him. Once a squad car came cruising down the block, he said, "Now let's go inside outta this cold." He turned for the building.

Nigga will be lucky if he find out he's disposable before it's too late, Playboy told himself introspectively as he trailed Gangsta, staring daggers at his back.

***

After Toni exchanged luggage with one of the couriers who ferried Milio's drugs and drug proceeds across the country in private jets, she headed out of the Mitchel International Airport.

As part of Toni and Milio's arrangement, Milio had shipments delivered to Toni. Over the past month, the couriers ran multiple keys of boy on the outgoing flight to Wisconsin, and tens of thousands of dollars on the return to Florida. Of course Milio couldn't send just anyone on a $30,000 flight across the States with luggage that contained kilos or tens of thousands of dollars in bundle bills.

Milio entrusted one of his two girls, Sasha and Angel, to fulfill the task.

Toni pulled the luggage to the Benz parked before the exit. Mateo awaited behind the wheel. She tossed the bag containing three bricks into the backseat before climbing inside the passenger's seat. Mateo pulled off en route to the expressway. He was careful to drive real smooth while ridin' dirty.

Traffic hadn't slowed yet, through snow started to fall as they drove. The forecasters had threatened more in a couple of hours, and they were glad to beat the worst of it.

"Now that I have an arrangement with Milio, I can flood the streets with my product. And I won't let no Nigga get in the way of me takin' shit over," Toni said. "Not even Diamond," she added firmly. Ty had let her know Diamond was outta lockdown, and Toni wanted to make him regret turning his back on her.

Milio kept his eyes on traffic and responded, "No matter how true that is, Toni, seems part of you still cares to be accepted by Diamond."

"No, Mateo, I only want him to respect me!" she retorted in a temper. "Diamond turned his back on the wrong bitch. Even after he was gonna kill me, I stayed loyal to his ass for too long. He and I were friends."

"And what if that just don't matter to him? What if now he only can consider you his enemy, huh, Toni?" Mateo played devil's advocate. He glanced over at her.

Toni gazed out the window at the passing vehicles. In in a lowered voice, she said, "Then I'd hate to have kill Diamond, but I wlll."

It was hard on Toni to get the respect she deserved in the streets being a female, and in order to get hers, she was willing to kill Diamond personally. And Gangsta and Banks had another thing coming if either of them thought they'd take over the game without killing her first. Toni was out to prove she was the baddest bitch in the game

Shifting in her seat towards Mateo, Toni tranquilly said, "Baby, I know all of this shit in the streets been distractin' me lately. But you should know that I'm here for you."

"Toni, I been thinking," Mateo said in a low voice.

"'Bout what?"

"Moving back home to Miami. And I want you to come with me." He planted a hand on her thigh.

Toni hesitated before offering a response. "I'ont know, Mateo, what about my operation? I put in too much work in the streets of Milwaukee to just up and leave now that I'm finally queen of shit."

"Which is exactly why you need to leave the streets to your crew. Let them put in the work while you reap the benefits. That way you can run your operation without getting your hands dirty while sheltered in a Little Havana mansion. You'd still have to go back and forth between cities for business. But for pleasure, Miami would be home," he reasoned.

Toni sat back in her seat and exhaled. "Look, Mateo, I need some time to think on it." She understood Mateo's reasoning. As long as she remained in Milwaukee, then her chances at dodging bullets and indictments were slim. However, she wasn't sure about moving, even though the drug trade did reduce the city to chaos.

Troublesome

Chapter 12

Tonight was the grand re-opening of Red Velvet, and shit was lit. Patrons had arrived en masse despite the weather. They were being asked fifty bucks for admission and that still didn't slow down the line outside. Many of the city's ballers were in the club.

Diamond - dripped in a Louboutin sweatshirt, a pair of biker jeans, and Louboutin boots, with shine in his ears neck and wrist - was in the second floor's VIP lounge. Throughout the night, many people welcomed Diamond home and he took it in stride. Standing near the balcony, Diamond overlooked the lively club scene.

On the main stage, Major preformed "Money Shower." Wearing a Balenciaga polo shirt, skinny jeans, and Balenciaga sneakers with sparkle that hung from his neck which most onlookers could only fantasize about the wealth that made such a thing possible, Major looked like established artist. There was a film crew following Major, shooting a video for "Money Shower", his first ever video shoot. While beautiful strippers surrounded him and dancing provocatively, Major rapped his raunchy lyrics into the camera, letting a handful of bills cascade over the twerking ass of a stripper. The music video would promote his song.

After Major cleared, the stage lights were dimmed as the newest main attraction, Mahogany, took the stage. Mahogany was a dark chocolate hue with small titties and a phat ass. She wore a long blond lacefront wig and cheetah print lingerie with black pumps. Seeing her up on stage reminded Diamond of Surprise. Though he never had any real feelings for her, part of him missed Surprise and how her presence used to breathe life in the club nightly.

"You did yo' thang on that stage, homie," Diamond said to Major as he stepped up.

"Fa sho'," Major replied. "Shit lit in here tonight."

"It isn't every night there's a grand reopenin'." Let's jus' hope the club don't get shut down anymore."

"Which is why that fuckin' Fed needs to be taken out before he can make another move."

"Agreed," Diamond replied. He took a drink from his glass of Hennessy.

Sarge approached. "Diamond, I'ont mean to ruin yo' night, but Toni jus' arrived wit' a crew. Said she wants to rap wit' you."

"Bitch must be crazy to bring her ass here tonight," Major growled.

"Me and my team can remove her if you want," Sarge suggested. He had security beefed up in case something went down tonight.

"Don't," Diamond told him, looking down from the balcony at Toni making it rain on Mahogany, who was pussy poppin' on a handstand. "I'll go and rap wit' her. Jus' keep an eye on her crew." He waved over a waitress with bottles of Don Perignon along with a message for Toni to meet him in his back office. Diamond then headed for the back of the club alone.

When Toni entered the office, she found Diamond positioned behind the desk. She noticed atop the desk with his drink and iPhone was the nickel-plated .45 in Diamond's reach. There was a tense stretch of silence as the two held one another's eyes.

Toni turned the bottle of Dom P up to her lips and then said, "I'm sure the champagne wasn't a peace offerin', but thanks anyway." In her Gucci hot pants jumpsuit and pair of knee-high Gucci boots with stiletto heels, she ambled up to the desk and perched herself against it, angled towards Diamond. "Welcome home."

Diamond leaned back in his seat, "Let's not forget it's because of you I was in lockdown," he reminded her.

"And it's also because of me yo' ass is out now," she shot back. "Diamond, recently Lynch came to me wantin' me to snitch on you."

"Sure you ain't here on Lynch's behalf, wearin' a damn wire?" he spat.

"Hell no, Diamond!" Toni jumped to her feet and slammed the bottle on the desk with a thud. Bubbly fizzed from the bottle. "I'd never betray you like that for nothin'!" she said, offended.

"Thought Pelle's ass would never betray me too. Had you not brought him around, then we wouldn't even be havin' this fuckin' problem."

"What more do you want from me, Diamond? I bodied Pelle and also got the money back he tried to run off with, all for you!" she cried out.

Diamond jumped to his feet and snapped, "Pelle deserved to be killed for his betrayal! And I'ont give a damn about the money!"

"I just don't understand how you can turn yo' back on me after all we've been through in the past." Her voice broke and he eyes misted.

Diamond made his way around the desk. "Toni, the past is the past," he replied gingerly. Diamond understood she meant more than just their past street affairs. In the past, he and Toni had had a thing for each other, and they slept together before Tywanna was around. But they decided not to take things further, although there was still something between them from their past.

"But Diamond, I——"

Diamond's iPhone vibrated on the desk. He and Toni peered down at the phone's display and saw the call was from Tywanna.

"She's good for you," Toni commented. She gently placed a hand on his arm. "I'm sorry she loss the baby. I know how much having a family means to you."

He exhaled. "I'm sure I'll have my own family one day."

"Diamond, I'm here for you," she told him.

"Look, Toni, you should jus' leave." He removed her hand from his arm. "And stay the hell outta my life." His tone was flat.

Toni threw her hands on her curvy hips. "You know what, Diamond? I don't need you. And I don't know why I even came here," she retorted. Toni grabbed the bottle of Dom P from the desk and then poured the champagne over Diamond's head before switching on her way out of the office, slamming the door behind her.

Diamond shook his head at how damn crazy Toni was. He wiped away the champagne with napkins.

There was a light rap on the door.

"It's open," Diamond called out and then Major entered, closing the door behind him.

"Noticed Toni and her crew bounce. Shit a'ight?" Major inquired.

Diamond returned to his seat behind the desk, letting out a deep breath. "Yeah. Toni just' felt a need to let me know that Lynch tried to have her snitch on me, but she wasn't willin' to."

"That still doesn't take away from the fact that she brought Pelle's snitch ass around. Diamond, you know how the game goes."

Diamond took a drink from his glass. "You right," he said evenly. But Toni showed and proved to him that she also respected the game. And as much as he thought he would, Diamond didn't feel the urge to kill Toni. Part of him hated the wedge between them.

"Look, Major," Diamond went on, "Why don't you go and enjoy yo'self while I take a moment."

Once Major exited the office, Diamond then grabbed his iPhone and called Tywanna.

***

Seated on the chaise lounge positioned before the plate-glass wall that overlooked the spectacular view of the snow-blanketed city, Tywanna was alone in the condo, drowning her sorrows in a bottle of Remy.

Since Diamond returned home, she'd been trying to find the confidence to tell him that she might not be able to give him a baby. Ty still faulted her mother for not saving their baby instead. Tywanna couldn't live with the thought of not being able to give Diamond the family he deserved.

Tywanna grabbed the prescription bottle of Vicodin off the end table. She opened the top, then poured out a handful of pills and swallowed them greedily. When the last pill snaked its way down her throat, she gulped down some Remy to make sure the pills stayed down. She then sank back into the chaise and awaited for death to claim her.

Ty's iPhone began to buzz on the end table. She grabbed for the phone, knocking over the lamp. She managed to grab the phone and she answered, noticing the call was from Diamond.

"Ty you there? Diamond called out, only hearing her breaths.

"D-Diamond, I'm s-sorry," she slurred through tears.

"Sorry about what, Ty?" He was concerned and confused.

"I'm sorry that I lost the baby."

"Listen, it's fine."

"I'm not willin' to live like this anymore," Ty murmured.

"Just hold on, Tywanna, I'm on my way to you," he told her, concern in his tone.

"I'm so sorry…" Ty's words trailed off and the phone fell from her hand onto the floor as the concoction of pills and liquor had her fading in and out of consciousness.

The phone call with Tywanna had Diamond concerned. He recognized that ever since she lost the baby she wasn't herself, and it bothered him that he couldn't seem to do much to help her. But Diamond wanted to be there for Tywanna.

Hurrying to his feet, Diamond pocketed his phone and stuffed the .45 on his waist as he made his way out of the office. Without bothering to inform Major or anyone, he hastily headed for the rear exit where his Porsche truck was parked out back. As he stepped outside, fat white flakes pelted down fit from the black sky as Diamond went for his ride. Diamond peeped a shadow figure approach. He saw him raise a gun, which glinted in the light from the street lamp. Diamond then reached for the .45 on his person.

"Don't even, Diamond," the gunman assertively warned. It was Gangsta.

Diamond lowered his hand away from his pistol and said, "I was expectin' you'd show up tonight to welcome me home."

"Well, here I am." Gangsta held the gun level on Diamond's some.

He quickly swept his eyes up and down the dimly-lit alleyway, finding it deserted. In order to see at all, he was forced to squint, to peer out through the narrowest of lash-shielded slits. Otherwise, the wind would've blinded him with his own tears.

Snow was coming down steadily, white and thick, dusting them and everything around them in white.

"Gangsta, I'm sure you don't give a fuck, but I need to get home to Ty," Diamond told him flatly.

"Heard that she lost the baby. And as much as I want you dead, you didn't deserve that," Gangsta expressed.

Diamond looked off down the alley. "What do you care, Gangsta?"

"Shoulda took Ty and moved away and got outta the game long ago," Gangsta said evenly.

"Why," Diamond brought his eyes back to Gangsta's, "so you can take over?"

Gangsta snorted. "Nigga, I'ma take over regardless. And it ain't shit you or Banks can do to stop me."

"Got word that Banks tried hittin' you up."

"Yeah. And I'ma make him regret even tryin'," he replied coldly.

"Gangsta, you seem to think killin' everyone is a means to an end."

"It's not about how many people you kill. It's who you kill that makes a difference," Gangsta told him. "And had you understood that, then maybe you woulda been smart enough to kill Lynch. You didn't realize it, but he's been out to get you for a while."

"Only reason I even dealt wit' Lynch was due to Balistrieri. And now that Balistrieri knows he's no good, Lynch is as good as dead," Diamond expounded.

"You know, Diamond, I admire yo' loyalty to that goop Balistrieri, even though I'ont like how he runs shit," Gangsta commented.

"Is that why you decided to betray and plug wit' that islander Yul?" Diamond replied bitterly.

Gangsta scoffed, "Yul's bad for business, so he and I are done."

"Figured that when you introduced me to him, which is why I didn't even consider acceptin' his business proposal."

"And now he wants you dead," Gangsta told him.

"Yeah, well, seems many men wish death upon me. Bother friends and enemies alike," Diamond breathed, glaring Gangsta in the eyes through the pelting snow.

"Unfortunately, in this game, money, power, and respect will turn a friend into an enemy," Gangsta replied unapologetically. He tightened his grip on the pistol, finna pull the trigger, when suddenly he peeped the Escalade crawling down the alleyway. He shoved Diamond into the show-shaded ground out of harm's way and shouted, "Get down!"

Blocka, blocka, blocka!

Prraat-prraat!

Once the Escalade had pulled up, Banks jumped out with a Tech 9 and let off, exchanging fire with Gangsta as Diamond went for his own weapon. Flames spat from the barrels of the firearms, lighting up the dim alley. Taking a shot in the side send Gangsta down, and Banks ran up with the Tech aimed on him.

Boom! Boom! Boom!

Diamond opened up on Banks before he could pull the trigger on Gangsta, causing Banks to turn the Tech on Diamond and return shots. Bullets whizzed by both Diamond and Banks narrowly. Banks began backpedaling for the Escalade as he and Diamond continued to trade fire. As Banks hurried inside the Escalade before he could pull the door closed, it sped off down the alleyway with Diamond filling it with holes.

When Diamond turned his weapon, going for Gangsta, he found Gangsta gone, leaving behind a trail of red snow.

Gangsta managed to make it to his getaway car, speeding away from the club. He was losing lots of blood and needed to get himself to a hospital. The slug he took in the side burned like hell and the pain was excruciating. He couldn't believe he'd taken a damn bullet for Diamond when he should've put a bullet in him instead. And he would. But first he wanted Banks.

Overhearing the shots fired, Major followed by Sarge and some of his security team came rushing out of the rear exit with guns in hand. They were just a moment too late, finding Diamond alone.

"You a'ight?" Major asked Diamond, concerned.

"Yeah. Shit coulda been worse," he answered, reflecting on Gangsta sparing his life.

"Hell happened?" Sarge wanted to know.

"It was Gangsta and Banks. Niggas came for me," he told them. "Look, I'ont have time to explain it right now. Gotta get home to Ty." He jumped into his Porsche truck and then shot down the alleyway.

Diamond white-knuckled the wheel as he sped on his way to check on Tywanna. He tried her phone twice with no answer. His mind was racing and heart pounding, not knowing what to take from the earlier call with Ty.

Arriving at the condo complex, Diamond slid the Porsche truck along the curb and parked. Arriving at the condo complex, Diamond slid the Porsche truck along the curb and parked. He then hurried out of the vehicle and into the building. Instead of the elevator, he ran up steps to the floor of the condo and rushed inside.

"Ty, where are you?" Diamond called out urgently as he made his way through the apartment. He found Tywanna on the love seat barely conscious and then rushed over to her, noticing on the floor at her feet an empty pill bottle and a partially-filled bottle of liquor tipped over. "What the hell did you do?" he asked desperately.

"D-Diamond, I-I'm sorry about our b-baby," she murmured.

"Don't worry about that right now, Ty. I gotta get you to a hospital." Diamond scooped her up in his arms and rushed her out to the Porsche. He sped for the nearest hospital, not letting the falling snow slow him down. Diamond wasn't ready to lose Tywanna.

***

After having her stomach pumped and being given fluids, Tywanna was in stable condition and just needed to detox. Fortunately enough for her, Diamond had rushed her to the hospital before the concoction of pills and liquor could turn fatal.

Diamond sat at Ty's bedside, holding her hand. He was so upset with her for attempting suicide, however, he was grateful that she was still alive. Diamond could not imagine losing Ty. He was sad enough he'd already lost his daughter. It pained him deeply, so he was sure it was hard on Ty.

"Diamond?" Tywanna called out in a whisper as she slowly opened her eyes.

"Diamond rose to his feet. "Tywanna, I'm glad you're okay. Was afraid I'd lose you too. Don't ever scare a nigga like that again. Hell were you thinkin'?" His tone was filled with relief.

"I'm sorry, Diamond. But you wouldn't understand," she replied in a low voice.

"Then help me to understand. What is it, Ty?" he urged.

Ty looked away out of the window at the flakes falling from the black sky and said, "The baby shoulda been saved instead of me. None of this would be if I hadn't gotten into a fight with mama over you and brung up my dad leavin' her. It's hard for me to live with the pain of it all."

"Ty, losin' the baby is no one's fault. And the next baby we have, we'll do our all to love it as much as we woulda loved Treasure," Diamond expressed.

Tears began to sail down Ty's cheeks. She met Diamond's eyes and cried, "Diamond, I...I may not be able to conceive anymore babies."

Tywanna's words pierced Diamond's heart. Now he further understood why she was taking the loss of their baby so hard.

"Why didn't you tell me this before, Tywanna?" Diamond inquired, barely audible.

"I-I was afraid that once you knew, then you would not care to be with me anymore since I may not be able to give you the family you want," Ty wept.

Diamond thumbed away her tears. "How can you think some shit like that?" he said, sounding disappointed. "That's no reason for me not to want you in my life anymore. Girl, I love you for you. Of course I want to have a baby wit' you. Although I'd rather have a life wit' you. The most important thing is we still have each other."

"But our baby..." Her words faded.

"She'll always be wit' us, Ty," Diamond promised. He leaned over and kissed her lips. "Look, I'ma go and get a nurse to check up on you."

As he turned for the door, Sandra was pushing it open and entering the room. Sandra placed a hand on Diamond's arm and said, "Thank you for calling me."

"No problem."

"I know she's still upset with me, but she and I really need to talk."

"Right. Jus' make sure you tell her the truth about her dad. She needs to know," Diamond told San, and she nodded. He departed the room.

Sandra stepped up to Ty's bedside and said, "I was so worried about you." She enveloped Ty in her arms.

"Mama, I'm so sorry." Ty's voice broke.

San gently planted a hand on her cheek. "Ty, I know losing the baby has been difficult for you to deal with. It was a difficult decision for me to have to make. But you must understand that your life is also precious, and that you deserve to live."

"I shoulda never faulted you or anyone for the loss of my baby. I'm really grateful that you decided to save my life and give me and Diamond a second chance, because I love him," she said through tears.

"Diamond's a really good man and he cares so much about you. I shouldn't have ever suggested you leave him. The two of you are meant to be. And I'm sure Diamond would've been a great father."

Ty hung her head. "And I was wrong for blamin' you for my dad leavin' us. It's just not havin' him in my life has always bothered me," Ty expressed.

In that moment, San knew and understood that Tywanna needed to know the truth about her father. She never realized that Ty had been so affected by the absence of her father, and San wanted her to know that if he could've been there, then he would have.

"Tywanna, sweetie," San started slowly. She took a seat in the chair at Ty's bedside. "There's something you need to know about your father."

Ty sat up in bed. "What is it, Ma?" she asked curiously.

Sandra took a deep breath. "Well, he didn't leave us. Actually, he was...was murdered," she unveiled.

"Murdered?" Tywanna was perplexed. "But why didn't you tell me the truth before?" She cared to know, her emotions everywhere.

"I'm sorry I didn't tell you the truth before, but at the time he was murdered, I felt you were too young to know that. I'm telling you the truth now because you need to understand that your father really did love you. I'm sure it's a lot for you to take in right now. I didn't mean to keep it from you. It's just time passed and I thought you'd learned to live with your father being gone. I just hope that you can forgive me."

Ty took a moment before responding. "Mama, I really wish you woulda told me the truth long ago. But I understand that you were only tryin' to protect me." She grabbed her mother's hand and expressed, "I forgive you."

Out in the corridor, after locating a nurse to check on Tywanna, Diamond was headed back towards the room. He stopped in his tracks when he saw Gangsta being wheeled into the recovery room through the closed glass door of the surgery hallway. He was with a doctor and nurses on either side of him, and lines were running into and out of him. A bag of blood under pressure was dripping into a line in his arm and the large white bandage covering his right side was stained pink. He looked as though he'd live, Diamond thought, and Gangsta didn't see Diamond there.

Diamond had spared Gangsta, his own thoughts a muddle of conflicting emotions. Why had he not allowed Banks to murk the nigga who sought his death? He was unwilling to acknowledge the tiny flicker of love for Gangsta that had begun to creep unhidden into his mind. He told himself that Gangsta would die, but at a time and a moment of his own choosing and after he had murked Banks.

Returning to the room, Diamond said, "The nurse says she'll be in to check on you shortly." He realized he'd walked in on Ty and San sharing a moment. "Are you two okay?"

"Yes. We are," San answered. She rose to her feet." Diamond, thank you for loving my daughter as much as I do."

"Believe me, I love her more than myself."

Tywanna grabbed Diamond's hand in hers and responded, "And I love you more than you know. Both of you."

"We know," San said. "Now we need you to promise us that you're done with abusing pills and liquor, Ty."

"Promise. I appreciate you both bein' here."

"Ty," Diamond began, "we'll be here no matter what."

Chapter 13

Seated on the sofa in the front room of their condo, Tywanna and Diamond watched *Love & Hip Hop* on the huge flat screen mounted on the wall in front of them. Ty lay with her head in Diamond's lap and he combed his fingers through her short hair.

Since bringing Ty home from the hospital, Diamond hadn't left her side, attending to her needs. He wanted her to know he was there for her, and she knew he was keeping a close eye on her out on her out of concern. However, both of them needed one another now more than ever before.

Diamond glazed at Ty, musing about how damn much she meant to him. Ty found him glazing down at her, and a sultry smile lifted the corners of her lips.

"Love, a nigga can't imagine livin' life wit'out you," Diamond crooned.

"Baby." Ty sat up and met his eyes. "I'll always be a part of your life." She pulled Diamond's lips to hers, and the two engaged in a passionate kiss. She climbed onto Diamond's lap, straddling him. He palmed her ass in both hands through her pajamas and gently bit on her neck and she tossed her head back, biting down on her lower lip.

Both of them were turned on. Diamond's dick was hard and pulsating and Ty's pussy wet and throbbing. He raised her crop top and slipped one titty then the other into his mouth, licking and sucking her erect nipples. She let out small moans, palming the back of his head, imagining the feel of his juicy lips and warm mouth massaging her clit.

A sudden loud rap on the front door brought their moment to a halt. Neither Diamond nor Ty was expecting any company, and the interruption was bad timing.

Raising from the sofa, Diamond said, "I'll get it. You jus' stay sexy for a nigga."

Ty admired the tent in his Gucci sweatpants before he turned for the door.

Annoyed by the interruption, without bothering to check the peephole, Diamond yanked open the door: "Toni?"

There was a stretch of balance between Diamond and Toni as they looked into each other's eyes.

"Baby, who's at the door?" Ty asked as she stepped up beside Diamond, finding Toni there. "Oh. Hey Toni."

"Hell are you doin' here?" Diamond question flatly.

"Diamond! Don't be so damn rude," Ty scorned him. She looked to Toni and said, "Girl, don't mind his ass. Why don't you come in?"

Once Toni entered the condo, Tywanna closed the door behind her. They all moved into the front room. Ty tried taking Toni's fur coat, but she declined.

"I won't be long, got Mateo waitin' on me in the car," Toni told her.

"Then why don't you make whatever you came here about quick," Diamond sniped.

Ty shook her head at Diamond. She turned to Toni and asked, "What brings you by?"

"Actually, I thought I'd drop by to check on you, Ty. Heard about your scare, and I just wanted to make sure you're okay."

Ty nodded. "Yeah, I'm fine. But it means a lot to me that you're concerned."

"Girl." Toni placed a hand on Ty's arm in solace. "You know I'll always be here for you if you need me."

"I know." Ty pulled her into her embrace, and over Ty's shoulder, Toni and Diamond met eyes.

Diamond pulled them apart and then snapped, "She don't need you, Toni, so how 'bout you jus' bounce!"

"Diamond, I'ont get why you turned yo' damn back on me, when all I've ever done was prove how fuckin' loyal I am to yo' ass!" Toni fired back.

"She's right, Diamond," Ty piped in. "After all you two have been through, Toni has never betrayed you. Diamond, Toni, you two deserve each other's loyalty."

Diamond knew Tywanna was right about Toni. He wiped away the tear they slid down Toni's cheek and tenderly said, "I know that I haven't shown it lately, but you mean a lot to me."

"Diamond, it hurts me how things have been between us lately 'cause I'm down for you. And I always will be," she vowed.

"I'm sure. And I'll never let anything else come between us," he pledged. Diamond kissed Toni on the forehead, and she found herself adoring it more than she expected.

"Look, I should leave y'all be. I'm sure Mateo's expectin' me by now," Toni said.

Diamond showed Toni out. He returned to the front room and then Ty wrapped her arms around his neck and he rested his hands on the small of her back.

"It was sweet of you to make up with Toni," Tywanna said.

"Thanks to you, she and I were able to do so."

"It was for the best," she told him. "Now, where were we before the interruption?" Ty pulled Diamond's mouth down onto hers, sharing a deep kiss.

***

Though the snow was no longer as thick on the ground, the city still glistened under the noonday sun. Mateo cruised the Benz through traffic. He noticed Toni seemed absentminded. Toni was reflecting on how things went back at Diamond and Ty's place. She was left with mixed emotions.

"Are you alright? You been awfully quiet since leaving Diamond's place. How'd it go back there?" Mateo inquired. He pulled to a stop at a red light.

"Turns out Ty's fine."

"I mean with Diamond," he clarified.

"Well, he wasn't feelin' that I was there to check on Ty. However, she was able to get Diamond to let bygones be bygones."

"So where does that leave things between you and he?" Mateo wanted to know. He understood how much Toni wanted to patch things up with Diamond.

I dunno." Toni peered out the window and quietly said, "Maybe now things can go back to normal between me and him."

"Toni, don't forget that Diamond had the mind to kill you," Mateo reminded her.

Toni shifted towards him in her seat. "I'm sure it ain't easy for you to understand, but after everything Diamond and me been through, I can't just forget about our past," she replied hostilely.

Looking over at her, Mateo said, "I just don't want you to get hurt again, okay?"

"Baby," she began with all hostility gone, "I do 'preciate your concern. But I won't let Diamond hurt me again." She looked deep into Mateo's eyes. "Even if that means killin' him."

Mateo exhaled deeply. "Fine, Toni." Once the light turned green, he pulled off with traffic and Toni sat back in her seat. He turned the Benz, heading west on Center Street. Moneybagg Yo's "Wit' Whateva" played in the background.

"Toni, have you thought at all about moving to Miami?" Mateo cared to know.

"Not much. I just don't know if I wanna up and move right now," she admitted.

He glanced over at her. "And what about me, Toni? I want to be close to Milio. But it seems like it's always about what you what," he responded in a temper.

"Mateo, baby, you know I'll do anything for you," Toni said tenderly. "And since you wanna move to Miami, then only for you, I will."

"Really?"

"Really," Toni smiled. She scooted towards Mateo, rubbing his dick through his skinny jeans. Her juicy lips kissed his neck as he felt her warm breath. Slowly, she slid her tongue up his neck to his right earlobe, which she bit on gently. This caused Mateo's dick to grow large and hard in her petite hand.

"I'ma suck you so damn good," Toni whispered into Mateo's ear as she undid his jeans and pulled out his hard dick. She then dived her head into his lap, taking his hardness into her warm mouth. Her head bobbed up and down in his lap. She sucked and rolled her tongue around the head of his joint.

Mateo gripped the wheel tightly, trying his best to avoid a collision while Toni sucked his dick greedily. "Damn babe, that's good," he groaned.

Toni continued sucking and slurping the pole as she reached to massage his balls with her hands. She took the stiff dick out of her mouth and licked all the way from the tip to the base, and then down to his balls. She put each of his balls in her mouth, swirling them with her tongue as she pumped his saliva coated dick with her hand.

Braking the Benz at a stoplight, Mateo allowed his head to rest back against the headrest as Toni licked the shaft of his piece up to its tip and then slid her warm mouth down on it to its base, deep throating him. Mateo's dick was pulsating and ready to explode! Toni's tongue lapped all around the swollen head of his piece as she stroked its shaft.

Mateo was on the verge of bustin' a nut when he noticed the Escalade draw up beside them, the passenger aiming a gun out the window at the driver side of the Benz. "T-Toni!"

Boc, boc, boc, boc!

Bullets peppered the Benz and the window of the driver's door imploded. As safety glass collapsed in a prickly mass across his chest and all over Toni, Mateo smashed down on the accelerator and the Benz zipped down the street. Had Toni not had her head ducked in Mateo's, lap then she would've gotten struck by bullets.

"Shit." Toni looked back over her shoulder through the rear window, finding the Escalade pursuing them, and noticed Ice. She hurriedly reached beneath her seat, and just as she came up with her mini-14 submachine gun, Ice sprayed the back of the Benz with bullets, shattering its rear window. Toni aimed her weapon out of the now-shattered rear window and opened up on the Escalade, hitting its front hood and windshield and causing it to swerve out of the line of fire.

Making a sharp turn, barely avoiding oncoming traffic, Mateo caused Toni to flop about. Once Toni recovered and planted herself in her seat, she checked the side mirror and saw the Escalade gaining on them, Ice in the front seat shouting something to Big Man as he fired shots. Then the mirror shattered and that whole scene vanished in a spray of tiny glass bits. Toni positioned herself to get a clean shot at the Escalade. She hung out the Benz and let the mini-14 ride sideways.

Prraat, prraat, prraat!

A hail of bullets Swiss-cheesed the Escalade, causing it to swerve and crash into a vehicle. Mateo weaved the Benz through traffic, taking a sharp turn at the corner, and Toni perpetually looked around to make sure they were no longer being pursued. Bending into the parking lot of a Checkers, Mateo parked in between two vehicles, out of view.

Toni shook her fuckin' head. "I'ma murk that nigga Ice whenever I catch his ass. Nigga don't know who he fuckin' with," she raved. She looked over at Mateo. He was slumped against the door, clutching his chest and breathing raggedly. "Mateo!" she cried out, noticing blood seep through the crevices of his fingers from the gaping hole in his chest. Toni used her hands to apply pressure to the bullet wound.

"T-Toni," he managed to get out. "I-I-I don't think I'm g-gonna make it." He coughed up blood.

"Don't think like that, baby. Just think about us movin' to Miami: how we'll enjoy the weather together, and how beautiful our home will be with an ocean view, and how Milio will love havin' us there," Toni urged.

Mateo mustard enough strength to lift his bloody hand to her cheek. "Milio t-told me that I d-did good for m-myself with you." He weakly smiled, blood trickling from the corner of his mouth. "Tell Milio...I l-love him."

"No, Mateo, you'll be able to tell him yourself. Just stay alive!" Tears rimmed her eyes.

Mateo began to have a coughing fit and gasping for air. Tears wet Toni's cheeks as she helplessly watched him pass away right before her eyes. She sat in her seat shedding tears in silence while staring into Mateo's dead, green eyes, pain and anger brewing within her. She loved Mateo and hated how his life ended. She couldn't help but imagine how the awful news would affect Milio.

Shortly thereafter, Diamond pulled up behind the shot-up Benz. Of all people, Toni only felt comfortable calling him to come get her. He had a way of making her feel secure in his presence. She didn't give many details over the phone, but Diamond heard it in her voice that she needed him. Toni leaned over and pecked a dead Mateo's cheek before departing the Benz. And once she stepped into Diamond's Porsche truck, he pulled out of the lot.

"You hurt?" Diamond asked out of concern. He noticed Toni covered in blood.

She slowly shook her head. "But Mateo…" Her voice faded as tears fell.

"Tonisha," he began in a low voice, "I'm sure you're hurtin' more than I know, and I wish there was somethin' I could say to ease it."

Toni shifted in her seat towards him. "Just say you won't hurt me again and mean it, Diamond," she urged, her tone emotional.

"I won't," Diamond told her. He glanced over at her, and added, "And I mean it."

***

Toni entered the suite of the Hilton hotel, finding Milio standing near the huge window with a forearm overhead supporting him against the pane. After receiving the devastating call from Toni about his kid brother's death, Milio had taken the first private jet out to Milwaukee along with his two girls, Sasha and Angel.

Grief consumed Milio. He couldn't imagine his kid brother dead. His grief was filled with rage and vengeance. He wanted Mateo's killer, although Milio knew it wouldn't ease the pain.

Milio stared out the window at the snow sifting from the night sky. He took a swig from his glass of Patron.

"Milio, are you okay?" Toni asked tenderly.

"I will be." He didn't bother facing her. "You know..." He spoke to Toni's reflection on the window pane. "I never imagined Mateo being murdered."

"And I can't imagine how you must feel. Had it not been for Mateo, then I woulda been murdered also. I can't apologize enough for what happened to him," Toni expressed.

Now Milio turned, facing her. "No need for your apologies. I just want the son of a bitch who's responsible for Mateo's murder. And I'm trusting you to avenge him, Toni Montana."

"And I will."

Chapter 14

Ashley knocked on the front door of Gangsta's loft. They hadn't spoken since he'd stormed out of her place behind their quarrel about Jade. She was there hoping she and Gangsta could make amends.

"Hey," Ash greeted Gangsta once he opened the door.

He hadn't been expecting her to drop by. Without a word, he let Ash inside and closed the door behind her. "Are you alright?" she asked out of concern, noticing the bloodstained bandage covering his side since he was shirtless.

"Nigga shot me. It's nothin' though," Gangsta told her as he took a seat on the sofa.

"Do you know who it was?" She sat beside him.

"Yeah, but that's not yo' concern. I'll deal wit' it myself."

Who shot him was more of her concern than he knew.

Gangsta went on, "What are you here about?"

"Actually, I came to apologize. I'ont like us not speakin' to each other," she admitted.

"Neither do I, Ash. But you need to let that Jade shit be. She and I are havin' a baby, and I want to respect that."

Ash sighed. "There's things you need to know about Jade."

Jade piped in, "And what about me?" she said, displaying attitude. Jade stood with her arms folded, only wearing Gangsta's tank top, near the bedroom door.

Ash jumped to her feet. "You know exactly what, Jade! Did you tell him the truth?"

"Truth about what?" Gangsta asked, puzzled. He rose to his feet.

Jade stood there silent.

"Go ahead, Jade, tell him," Ash insisted.

"Hell is she talkin' 'bout, Jade?" he eagerly wanted to know.

"Gangsta, it's nothin'," Jade stammered.

"Since you won't tell him the truth, then I will," Ash piped in. "Gangsta, the baby may not be yours. Instead, it may be Banks's. I tried tellin' you she's been fuckin' him behind your back, but you just wouldn't listen."

Gangsta glared at Jade. "Is it true?" he questioned in a gruff tone.

"Tell him, Jade," Ash pressed.

"Ashley, leave us be, a'ight?" he told her firmly.

With no further words, Ash eyed Jade sharply before making her way out.

Jade peered down at her bare feet. "Gangsta, I——"

"Is the shit true? Huh?" His tone was cold.

"Um, n-no."

"You know what? Call the nigga," Gangsta told her.

"But Gangsta, I——"

"Shut da fuck up and call the nigga. Now!" he demanded.

"Okay, Gangsta, damn," Jade caved. Reluctantly, she stepped over to the coffee table, grabbed her iPhone out of her bag, and then dialed Banks. "I'm callin'."

"On speaker," he insisted.

Jade set the call on speaker phone then set the phone on the coffee table.

After a couple of rings, Jade said, "His ass ain't even an-swerin'——"

"Bitch, don't you dare touch that phone," Gangsta warned, pre-venting Jade from ending the call.

A few rings later, Banks answered. "Told you I'd call you when I feel like getting my dick sucked, Jade."

Gangsta backhand smacked the hell outta Jade, knocking her onto the floor. "Can't believe you really been fuckin' that nigga be-hind my back, knowin' I got beef wit' his ass. Ain't no tellin' what else you been doin'. Prolly was fuckin' Diamond, too," he raged.

"Gangsta!" she said, offended.

"Keep my damn name off yo' dick-suckin' lips."

Jade picked herself up off the floor. Her right eye had begun to immediately swell and discolor from the backhand smack. "It ain't even like that," she cried.

"Did you tell that nigga the baby's his too?" Gangsta demanded to know. Judging by her silence, he figured her answer. "You know what, hoe? You ain't shit. Get the fuck outta my face." He grabbed a fistful of her tracks and pulled her to the door, shoved her out into the hallway, and then slammed the door shut.

Gangsta stepped over to the sofa and plopped down. *How could that hoe let me believe the baby was mine when all along, of all niggas, it's also possibly Banks's?* he contemplated. He didn't know whether to be hurt or mad. Apparently he owed Ash apology because she'd been trying to tell him Jade was no good.

"Yo Gangsta," Banks called out over the speakerphone, having overheard everything. "Neva trust a bitch that'll fuck you for some purses," he scoffed.

Snatching up the phone, Gangsta retorted, "Nigga, you can have the punk bitch Jade. She fuck around and be the reason you get smoked."

"I'ont beef over no bitch, so don't let that be the reason. You already know what it is when I catch you," he forewarned.

"Real shit, you shoulda finished me off the night at the club. Now I'm comin' for you. Hard!"

"You'd be finished if it wasn't for Diamond. Don't be slackin' in these streets, Gangsta," Banks told him in a threatening manner.

"I keep mine, "Gangsta assured.

"Give Jade my best – if you can." Banks killed the call.

Jade was pounding on the door, pleading for her belongings. Gangsta snatched up her bag off the coffee table and then steamed over to the door, ripping it open. Jade jumped back, startled. Carelessly, Gangsta tossed Jade's things at her bare feet before slamming the door in her face.

***

Night was falling when Ashley got home. She parked and cut off the engine of her Chrysler Sebring. Her iPhone chimed a text. She reached over into the passenger's seat for her Hermes bag and fished out the phone, then saw the text was from Gangsta.

Hell could his ass want? Ash asked herself introspectively with a scoff. She checked the message:

Gangsta//8:17 p.m.
Lil sis, u were right about Jade.
My bad for not listenin' to u.

Ashley shook her head and texted him in reply.
Ash//8:19 p.m.
SMH. Yo' bad is right. I just couldn't let that hoe play u.

Gangsta//8:20 p.m.
'Preciate that u care.

Ash//8:21 p.m.
Always. Now what about Jade?

Gangsta//8:23 p.m.
If the baby's mine I'll take care of it. But Fuck Jade, I'm done with that hoe.

Ash//8:25 p.m.
Still can't believe she would fuck Banks behind yo' back. And by fuckin' on him she disrespected Lexi. SMDH

Gangsta//8:26 p.m.
Jus' so u know, Banks is the one who shot me. And it has to do w/ Lexi.

Ash//8:26 p.m.
What?!

Gangsta//8:27 p.m.
I'll explain it all to u the next time we see each other.
TTYL.

Ashley rested her head back against the headrest. She mused about Gangsta mentioning being shot by Banks, puzzled by what it could have to do with Lexi. With that thought weighing heavy on her mind, she exited the car. Ash was looking forward to the next time she'd see Gangsta in order to get some answers.

***

Walking through the cemetery, Tywanna headed for her father's gravesite. Her mother had offered to come along with her, but Ty felt the need to alone. She needed to see for herself that her father was dead and gone.

Arriving at her father's headstone, Ty's heart grew heavy with sorrow, thinking about being robbed of knowing him in the flesh. She couldn't help but wonder how it would have been for her growing up with him in her life. Tears welled up in her eyes as she thought about how she missed out on her father's love. Believing he had left her and her mother caused Ty to resent him, up until Sandra decided to tell her the truth about him actually being murdered. And now Ty was interested in knowing more about her father. All Sandra had told her aside from his name, Cassius, was that he was a good man. Ty was sure there was much more to him than her mother cared to speak of.

Hearing approaching footsteps from behind, Ty peered back over her shoulders and found Banks. She immediately pulled her .380 out of her Chanel bag and aimed at Banks, stopping him in his tracks.

"Take it easy, will you?" Banks suggested.

"Are you followin' me? 'Cause it's beginnin' to seem like it," Ty breathed. She knew that Banks had it out for Diamond, so maybe he was there to harm her instead, she thought.

"No," Banks snorted, "I ain't followin' you."

"Then what are you doing here?"

"Could ask you the same. But if you must know, I come here from time to time to visit this gravesite. He was my pops. How do you know him?" he asked curiously.

Tywanna lowered the gun, eyeing him in disbelief. "He was also my dad," she told him in a quiet voice.

Stepping up to the headstone, Banks looked down at its engravings and said, "Always wondered who the second child mentioned on the headstone was." He met Ty's eye. "Now I know."

Neither of them knew what to think in that moment. Tywanna was still trying to grasp the fact her father was actually deceased, and now she suddenly learned that she had a brother who, of all people, turned out to be Banks. And for Banks, he never expected that if he did have a sister, it'd be Ty. They each possessed mixed thoughts on their situation.

"But," Ty began slowly, sounding puzzled, "my mother never mentioned he had another child."

"Maybe she never knew."

"Does your mother know?"

Banks looked off in the distance towards the brilliant sun. It was odd, still feeling cold sun so bright overhead.

"My mother's dead," he replied in a lowered vice. "OD'ed on heroin when I was a shorty."

"Oh. Sorry."

"It's cool. You didn't know."

"What about our dad? Do you remember him well? Apparently he was murdered when I was too young to even remember."

"No, I don't remember him either. But growin' up wit'out a father's somethin' you never forget," he said.

Ty understood what he meant.

"What now, Banks? I mean, now that we know we're siblings, what'll come of us?" Tywanna wanted to know.

Banks shook his head. "I'm not sure."

"And what about you and Diamond?"

Banks snapped his eyes back to hers and firmly said, "Us bein' siblings doesn't change a damn thing between me and Diamond. Already told you our beef has nothin' to do wit' you, Ty."

"Neither did it have anything to do with Lexi, but look at what happened to her! Would it matter to you if I also lost my life behind whatever beef you and Diamond have? Huh, Banks?" she shouted in a temper.

"Believe me, I hate what happened to Lexi. And I don't want it to happen to you. But my problem's wit' Diamond, not you," he told her.

"And like I told you before, Banks, if you got a problem with Diamond, then you have one with me," Ty retorted. She raised the pistol at his chest.

"I respect that you're down for Diamond. But are you willin' to kill your blood brother for him?" Banks stared into her eyes as he breathed in the cold air. He felt anger rise in his gut as he waited, wondering if she'd pull the trigger. He turned, walking away, ditching her to let him go or shoot him in the back.

She lowered the gun and let him go.

Apparently Tywanna wasn't willing to kill her blood brother. But she knew that Diamond wouldn't think twice about doing so. How would she tell Diamond that Banks, his arch enemy, was her blood brother?

***

The Rolls Royce came to a stop at the deserted train tracks. Frank was there to meet with Lynch. While Alphonse remained behind the wheel with his eyes peeled for any sign of trouble, Little stepped out and frisked Lynch before allowing him into the rear seat of the Rolls, where the mob boss awaited, smoking a stogie.

"You look like hell, Agent," Frank commented, noticing Lynch was unkempt more than usual and hadn't seemed to groom in several days.

Ignoring the comment, Lynch stated, "I'm done playing by your rules, Frank. The only one who seems to win is you. Well, not anymore, dammit."

"Agent." Frank took a drag of the cigar. "Does this have to do with you taking out attempts on my life?" He blew out a cloud of smoke. "Yeah, I know all about it. At first I couldn't understand who'd have a reason to come after me, until I realized it had be a very desperate man. Not to mention Diamond brought things to my attention as well.

Lynch eyed him sharply. "Yeah, well, Diamond's bound to be your downfall. Trust me, he——"

"No, I don't trust you, Agent!" Frank boomed, cutting him short. "Unlike you, Diamond has never betrayed me. If anyone, you're who's bound to be my downfall."

"And if I have to, then I'll take us both down," Lynch threatened, and Frank understood he was referring to confessing about the murder of two cops Lynch executed for him.

"Only reason I haven't gotten you whacked yet--"

"Is because you need me for supply, Frank," Lynch interjected. "Which is exactly why from now on you will play by my rules."

Frank leaned back against the soft leather seat, his eyes fixed on Lynch. "Alright, I'm listening, Agent."

"Then listen close. From now on, I want 60% of all proceeds gained by drug distribution," Lynch told him in a demanding tone.

"Have it your way." Frank puffed the cigar.

"And Frank, I advise you to follow my rules or else," Lynch warned. He pushed open the door, fixing to step out of the vehicle into the cold.

"Agent," Frank called, out halting Lynch. "Any fool can make a rule and every fool will mind it," he quoted.

Lynch proceed to step out and then slammed the door shut with a thud.

Lynch failed to realize that Frank was no longer in need of his services. Immediately after Frank learned of the agent's betrayal, he made other arrangements in order to supply his franchise. But he decided to play those cards close to his chest, and now that Lynch exposed his own cards, Frank knew how to play him.

Alphonse lowered the partition between the front and back seats.

Little looked up in the rearview mirror, catching Frank's eye. They sought their boss's order.

"Ease up, fellas. That son of a bitch will get his, even if I have to blow him to pieces." Frank puffed the cigar.

Chapter 15

Moonlight reflected off the white snow and helped light Banks's way. He was thankful the streets were clear of ice and he could rocket his Ashton toward another one of his trap spots, his music blasting Meek Mill's "Respect the Game".

Banks yielded the whip at a stoplight. He checked the mirrors for any suspect vehicles, finding none. Being caught slacking on the streets could cost him his life, which is why he rode with a pistol in his lap. With all the beef in the streets, Banks knew he needed to be ready to shoot first and ask questions later.

Just so happened, Banks spotted the Porsche truck which belonged to Diamond. *Must be my lucky fuckin' day*, his conscience suggested. The Porsche coasted by him across the intersection. Banks cut the music before he committed an illegal turn, cutting off traffic and causing motorists to blast their horns as he pursued the Porsche-truck.

He needed Diamond dead so that he could make major moves in taking over the drug trade in the streets. And had it not been for the bitch-ass nigga Gangsta, then Banks would have bodied Diamond the night at Red Velvet. Needing Diamond dead, Banks wouldn't hesitate to air-out his Porsche.

Nigga don't even know what's comin', Banks said to himself introspectively. One hand on the wheel and the other gripping the Glocks .40 in his lap, Banks wove through traffic, pursuing the Porsche as it darted eastbound down Locust Street. Up ahead, the Porsche's brake lights glowed as it yielded to a stop at a stoplight. Banks dipped the Aston around a vehicle and then pulled up on the passenger's side of the Porsche truck. He extended an arm out of the window, aiming his weapon on the Porsche.

Banks hesitated. He didn't expect the passenger's seat to be occupied by Tywanna. The held one another's eyes, hers filled with uncertainty and his with perplexion. Ty slowly shook her head "no", and reluctantly Banks withdrew the weapon. The light flipped green and then Diamond, who was oblivious to what was going on as he bobbed his head to the music, dispelled.

Banks remained braked at the light. He slammed a fist down on the steering wheel out of frustration. In that moment, he didn't know what the hell came over him. Banks found it difficult to admit that he just couldn't bring himself to squeeze the trigger on the strength of Ty.

A car horn blared behind Banks, bringing him to realize he was holding up traffic. He then pulled off, making a right turn and heading towards his original destination. Banks rode in silence, his thoughts drifting in the air.

Subsequent to checking in on the trap spots, Banks headed for his Aston. At the curb sat his whip, gleaming in the cold snow. He reached the driver's door, pulled it open, and began to step inside.

"Say Banks," a voice called out from behind and halted Banks.

Discretely, Banks placed a hand on the butt of the Glocks .40 on his waist, ready to go out bustin'. Peering back over his shoulder, he found a familiar face in Smooth. He removed his hand from the pistol and said, "Thought you was some nigga tryna catch me slackin'."

"Ain't even like that," Smooth replied. "Been tryna find you for a while now."

"And how'd you know to find me here?" Banks insisted on knowing. He noticed Smooth's hand was in a cast courtesy of it being smashed by Tate.

"Tina told me she sees you here often."

"Yeah, I know Tina. She's a regular fiend at this spot."

"Used to be one of my hoes. Back before she became a dope-fiend. Speakin' of, I wanna rap wit'chu 'bout yo' moms and pops," Smooth mentioned.

Banks's expression turned serious. "Hell do you know about my parents?"

"Mind if we take a ride under some heat? I'll tell you what I know," Smooth suggested.

Banks jerked his head towards the Aston and then he, followed by Smooth, entered the whip. Once they were inside, Banks pressed the push to start button and the car purred to life. He then pulled off.

"Now," Banks began, lowering the volume of the music, "Tell me what it is you know about my parents."

"When I was last in Magic Clippers, I overheard you ask Tate about yo' pops before he smashed up my damn hand. And only over two fuckin' grand. Can you believe that! As long as I been knowin' his ass and as much money as I——"

Banks snapped his fingers a few times, cutting off Smooth's rant. "Take that shit up wit' Tate. Right now I jus' wanna know about my parents," Banks told him.

"Well, I knew yo' moms and pops from back in the day. In fact, I introduced them. You see, young blood, Cash had a thing for yo' moms, Precious, but he had to go through me to get wit' her since she was one of my hoes. No offense."

"None taken. So, you introduced my parents. What's the point?" Banks urged as he zoomed through a yellow light.

"After Cash and Precious started to see each other exclusively, yo' moms decided to retire her hoe boots. Yo' pops took her in. But Tate had a problem wit' it," Smooth told him.

"What does any of this has to do wit' Tate?" Banks glanced over at him, curious.

Smooth shifted in his seat towards Banks. "Thing is, Tate thought yo' folks bein' together was gettin' in the way of Cash runnin' the game how he expected. So Tate tried to convince him to leave Precious, but Cash wasn't havin' it. Then Tate decided that before he'd allow Cash to be his downfall, he'd rather put a bullet in him," Smooth revealed.

Abruptly Banks veered the car to the curb. He then snatched Smooth by his coat, grabbed the pistol from his own lap, and pressed its muzzle to Smooth's jaw. "How the fuck would you know, huh?" he raged.

Smooth swallowed the lump in his throat. "Even after Precious left my stable, she and I remained in touch. She told me everything she knew after Cash was killed. She also told me that once she confronted Tate about it, he forced her to shoot dope in order to use it to control her," he stammered, not making any sudden moves.

"So you mean to tell me that Tate's the reason both of my parents are dead?" Banks said disapprovingly. "I'ont believe you."

"Believe me or not, I'm tellin' you the damn truth!" Smooth cried out.

"Maybe you jus' tryna use me to get back at Tate for smashin' yo' fuckin' hand." Banks applied more pressure of the muzzle to Smooth's jaw and demanded, "How come you didn't tell me any of this shit before?"

"'Cause up until I overheard you at the shop, I didn't even know Cash and Precious were your folks," Smooth explained, stammering.

"Tate's been like family to me since I lost both parents. He took me in and practically raised me." Banks was unable to wrap his head around the possibility of Tate being the cause of his parents' deaths.

"Maybe Tate has been there for you outta guilt. But if he finds out you know about your folks, Tate will kill you too," Smooth forewarned.

Banks let go of Smooth's coat and withdrew his pistol.

"Look, I'll jus' get out here." Smooth pushed open the door.

"Smooth," Banks called in a low, callous voice, halting Smooth as he went to step out the car. "If none of what you told me is true..." He pressed the barrel to Smooth's chest.

The muffled shots were fatal. Smooth's body slumped out of the car onto the sidewalk blanketed with snow. Banks sped away from the curb down the street.

Banks's head was spinning. The thought of losing his parents at the hands of Tate was all too much. He didn't know if any of what he was told held some truth, however, he intended to find out.

With thoughts rolling around in his head, Banks rocketed the Aston aimlessly through the moonlit streets.

***

"Smells good in here, "Diamond commented as he stepped into the kitchen of the condo, where Tywanna was preparing dinner. He stepped up behind Ty, who was standing at the island prepping a dish of lasagna, and wrapped his arms around her torso. "You a'ight? Been quiet since we got home."

"Yes, baby, I'm alright," Ty replied, fixing a smile at him at him over her shoulder. Quiet as kept, she was distracted by the thought of Banks.

Diamond pecked her on the corner of her lips. "Good. 'Cause I was beginnin' to worry about you. Jus' know that you can talk to me about anything," Diamond told her. He began planting small kisses on Ty's neck and caressed her curves.

"Baby, would you stop and lemme get this dish in the oven," Ty cooed.

"That shit can wait." Diamond turned her facing him, and then kissed her lips. He thought she looked like a snack wearing black yoga pants and an oversized Chanel sweatshirt that hung off one shoulder, showing a black bra strap, and big fuzzy slippers.

Tywanna's cell began ringing in the distance from the living room. "Diamond, why don't you help me and put this dish in the oven while I go and answer that?" she said.

"I got'chu." Diamond slapped her on the ass as she headed for the living room.

Ty grabbed her iPhone from the glass end table. She checked its display, surprised that it read "Lexi". She stared at the iPhone's display in wonder. Reluctantly, she answered the call and remained silent with an ear to the phone

"Tywanna, are you there? It's me, Banks."

In a lowered voice so Diamond couldn't hear her, she said, "Yeah. I'm here. But why are you calling from Lexi's phone?"

"I need to talk wit'chu, and I was sure yo' number was saved in Lex's phone. Found it hard to get rid of her phone for some reason," he told her.

"I understand. It's hard for me to erase her number." Ty admitted. "But what do need to talk to me about? Thought you wanted nothin' to do with me." She snorted.

"Well, you thought wrong."

"How else…" Realizing she began to raise her voice, Ty restrained herself. She lowered her voice again. "Banks, how else am I s'posed to think when you got a problem with Diamond?"

"Like I told you before, my problem's wit' Diamond?"

Diamond called out to Tywanna from the kitchen. "Love, the dish is in the oven. Anything else I can help you wit'?"

"Um, no, thank you," Ty called back. She made her way towards the balcony.

"I take it that's Diamond." Banks spoke the name with a scoff. "Does he even know you're my li'l sis yet?"

"Please, you don't know me well enough to call me your li'l sis, so don't," Ty told him as she stepped out onto the balcony, pulling the glass slide door nearly closed. "And I'm sure Diamond doesn't care to hear anything about you."

"Maybe it's best that you tell him sooner rather than later so he doesn't feel betrayed," Banks suggested. He realized how difficult it must be for her to have to tell Diamond they were siblings.

"Look, I'll tell you whenever I'm ready," she said, sounding agitated. Ty looked at the half moon overhead. It looked as cold and hard as the solid mountains of snow that blanketed everything around her: trees, street signs, cars, mailboxes. "Now, what exactly do you need to talk to me about?"

"Banks exhaled heavily. "It's about our pops."

"What about him?" Ty urged. She was as interested as Banks in knowing more about her father.

"I may know who murdered him," he told her.

"And who might it be?"

"Tate, the man who practically raised me." He sounded disappointed. "And that's not all. He also may have forced my mom into becomin' a damn dopefiend."

"Oh my God, that's awful!" Ty gasped. "And what makes you think he may have done any of it?"

"An old pimp who knew our pops in the days thought is best to tell me what he claims is true. Claims Tate offed our pops in order to take over his operation, and used dope to control my moms," Banks expounded.

"I'm sure it's very hard on you to deal with the claims of losin' both your parents due to the man who raised you. But you need to find out the truth,"

Banks sighed. "I don't know what I'll do if it's true Tate betrayed my parents."

"Banks, what a man is willin' to do isn't said; it's done," Tywanna told him."

"Facts," Banks concurred.

There was a moment of silence.

"I need to know, Banks," she began slowly. "Earlier today when you had the chance, why didn't you pull the trigger?"

"Same reason you didn't pull the trigga when you had the chance, Tywanna," he answered evenly. "Whether we like it or not, we're brother and sister. And on the strength of that, there should be mutual respect between you and me."

"Maybe you're right."

"Look, I gotta go. 'Preciate the talk."

"We can talk whenever you feel the need to," Ty offered.

"I'll keep that in mind," Banks assured her before disconnecting the call.

Tywanna admired the postcard beauty all around her, the city covered with white as far as the eye could see. She wondered how life would have been growing up knowing Banks was her brother, if it would have changed the way things were between her and Diamond. She didn't know how to let Diamond know that Banks was her sibling. However, she hoped that she could be the reason her long-time lover and long-lost brother made peace

"There goes my baby," Diamond said as he slid open the slide door of the balcony. "Started to wonder where you were."

Ty stepped up to him and wrapped her arms around his neck. "Let's go back inside and finish cookin' dinner."

"How 'bout we jus' skip to dessert." Diamond grinned down at her.

***

Hell does Banks want with me out here this damn late? Tate mused as he parked his Jaguar.

It was nearly midnight when Tate arrived at Lincoln Park, where Banks had insisted they meet. Banks phoned Tate, telling him they needed to have a discussion, and Banks was adamant about them having it in person. This had Tate curious as to what it was Banks needed to discuss. Whatever it was Tate just hoped it wouldn't get in the way of his operation.

Before stepping out the Jag, Tate tucked his .357 Magnum in his waist. He found Banks standing near the lagoon, peering out at the ice-sheathed water.

"Banks," Tate called out as he stepped up beside him, "what in the hell is this about?"

"It's about my pops," Banks told him while he remained peering out at the glistening ice covered lagoon.

Tate hesitated. "Look, I told you everything there is to know about yo' old man," he said evenly.

Meeting his eyes, Banks replied, "Except one thing. You never told me who murdered him." He observed Tate's face to measure the impact of his words.

Tate held a bold face. "Look, Banks, I wish I could tell you that, but I can't."

"Maybe that's because he was murdered by you," Banks retorted gruffly. "Is that true? Don't lie to me."

Tate scoffed then shook his head. "Truth is, I am the one who murdered Cash," he revealed in an even tone, "But only because his ass was becomin' too careless and seemed to be goin' soft on me and shit. Cash had started lettin' shit that doesn't even matter get in the way," he added resentfully.

"I take it you mean my damn moms," Banks snarled. Rage was brewing within him.

"I don't know what Cash seen in her. Precious wasn't shit but a gold-diggin' hoe. And she trapped Cash by gettin' pregnant with you. Too damn bad she let the H get the best of her," Tate said bitterly.

Banks was consumed by rage. "And I thought Smooth had only told me this jus' to turn me against you."

"I shoulda put a bullet in Smooth's ass a long ago," Tate snorted.

"Well, I did it for you, 'cause I didn't believe Smooth. But turns out he ain't the one who deserve a bullet from me," Banks sniped. "Can't believe you're the v reason why my pops and moms are dead,"

"Banks," Tate began tenderly. "I took you in and raised you. I taught you everything to know in the streets so you could survive. I treated you like family," he stressed.

"Loyalty makes people family, Tate! But all you are is a betrayer!" Banks raged. "And bein' that you betrayed my pops in order to take over the operation, I'm takin' it back. And I demand you leave this city, never to return. Or, by pops' grave, I'll murder you, Tate," he solemnly swore.

Tate turned his back to Banks, looking over the icy lagoon, and in a lowered voice he said, "So this is what it comes to?" He discreetly pulled the .357 from his waist. "You know, I realized you'd find out the role I played in yo' folks' deaths sooner or later. My only regret is not killin' you before——" Suddenly Tate spun on his heels, raising his gun.

Blocka!

Before Tate knew it, he was staring down the barrel of Banks's .40 Glock. The spark from Banks's pistol illuminated the darkness, revealing the look of regret on Tate's face at the pull of the trigger. The bullet forced a hole through Tate's forehead and he did an ungraceful pirouette. He fell on the ice, breaking it, and sank to the bottom of the lagoon.

Banks turned and walked away with no regret of his own.

**

"Tate will no longer be the head nigga in charge. From now on, I will be," Banks announced to the crew that once belonged to Tate.

Magic Clippers was closed for business this morning. After offing Tate last night, Banks wanted to set it straight that he was now large and in charge and willing to keep it that way by any means.

While seated in the barber's chair getting his fade touched up, Banks observed the crew members before him. Standing on his right was Ice, and Big Man occupied the barber's chair on his left.

Banks continued, "And to set shit straight, yeah, I murked Tate. Nigga had it comin'. If any of you have a problem wit' it, then do whatever you think is necessary. Either you wit' me or against me," he stated assertively, looking into the crowd of faces.

Whether it be out of fear or respect, none of the crew objected to Banks's takeover. However, Dub was seething. Tate has been his long-time friend, so Dub wasn't accepting that Banks had killed him. And when the moment came, then Dub would get even.

After a stretch of silence from the crew, Banks said, "If any one of you ever betray me, then you best be ready to do or die."

Once the barber finished up Banks's haircut, he then stepped over to the mirror to check himself out. *Damn, I look like my fuckin' pops*, Banks mused. Through the reflection of the mirror, which gave him a view out of the shops' front picture window, Banks peeped the red G-Wagon crawl to a hair in the street before Magic Clippers. And hanging out from the G-Wagon's window, aiming a Draco, was Gangsta.

"Oh, shit!"

Boc! Boc! Boc! Boc! Boc!

A deadly fusillade of bullets peppered the interior of the shop, finding marks and leaving bullet holes in the walls. Bullets tore through most everyone and everything they encountered. The rapid gunfire kept those who managed to hit the floor pinned down as bullets whizzed by overhead. Once the 150-round drum of the Draco was emptied, the G-Wagon peeled away with tires screeching.

A second before the shots erupted, Banks and some others were able to duck for cover. He reluctantly rose to his feet. Taking a look around, he found some of his crew maimed and a few bodied. Dub had caught a bullet in the arm. He then turned and found Ice standing near a bullet-riddled Big Man, who was slumped to the side in the barber's chair, with four bullet holes in his torso and two in the face.

Banks stepped up beside Ice and said, "We gon' get that nigga Gangsta."

Troublesome

Chapter 16

"Mmm, yeeess, baby, it feels so damn good!" Ashley moaned erotically while she rode Major's dick. She grinded on him and her small titties jiggled. Leaning forward, Ash gently bit Major's lower lip.

Her body began to quiver and moans grew louder as a curve of orgasm took its course. Palming her ass, Major slammed Ash up and down on his stiff dick, sliding deep inside her slippery slit. A nut swelled up in the tip of his rod.

"Damn, boo!" Major grunted as he came.

Ash rolled beside him in bed. The couple was covered in perspiration and panting from good fuckin'.

Ash had awakened Major with small kisses, which led to their morning sex. Since Major spent many days and nights at the studio, they took advantage of the time they were afforded.

"Ash, we need to talk," Major said.

She snuggled up on him. "About?"

"'Bout my rap career. I want you to be the first to know that I'm gonna sign a contract with Gucci Mane's record label, So Icey Entertainment."

"Congratulations, Major, I'm happy for you!" Ash beamed excitedly. "You been workin' so hard at this and you deserve it."

"'Preciate it." His tone was flat.

"Thought you'd be excited about this."

Major sat up in bed. "Believe me, I am."

"Well, I can't tell," Ash commented. She propped herself up on an elbow "What's the matter, Major?"

He let out a heavy breath. "Been thinkin' about movin' to Atlanta," Major told her.

"Why do you need to move there?" Ashley wanted to know.

"I believe it'll be a good move for my rap career. It'll give me the opportunity to be around Gucci Mane while he schools me to the hustle side of the music game and the business side of the industry," he expounded.

"But your whole life is here."

"And I'm chasin' my rap dreams in order to get outta this life as I know it. And I wanna take you and the twins wit' me," Major expressed.

Ashley reflected on it a moment. "Major, I support your dream. Really, I do. But I need to think about movin' with you. How about you go out to Atlanta so you can focus on your career and get yourself established, then we'll figure it out," she suggested.

"I'd rather not go wit'out you, Ash."

"It's what's best for you right now. And I want the best for you more than anyone," she said sincerely.

Major leaned over and kissed her lips. "That's why a nigga love yo' ass so much."

"I know," Ash smiled. She rolled out of bed and purred, "Now come show me just how much you love my ass in the shower." She headed into the adjacent master bathroom, and Major followed her nakedness.

***

The door chimed.

The pregnant woman, Felicia, wobbled to the front door of the lower duplex home. She was home alone and wasn't expecting company. Peeking from behind the window blind, she saw a woman on the porch who she didn't recognize. *Must be another side bitch lookin' for my man*, she mused resentfully.

Disengaging the locks, Felicia pulled open the door, and said, "Can I help you?"

"Bitch, you can start by losin' the attitude, then tell me where the fuck Ice is," Toni demanded. She touched the button on the handle of the knife in her hand. The spring-head blade popped into sight; it was seven inches long, thin, and nearly as sharp as a razor. And in a blur, she brought up the knife and lightly pricked Felicia's throat with the point of the blade.

Felicia's dark brown eyes were very wide. She'd had the breath knocked out of her and could not scream. Her gaze traveled down

148

to Toni's fist and to the handle of the knife. She wondered who the crazy bitch was looking for Ice.

Felicia was Ice's baby mama. She had been with him for two years now and loved him maybe more than she should, even though he beat on her and cheated on her regularly. But she knew he loved her too, after all.

"If you try to scream for help, I'll push this knife straight into yo' damn throat. I'll ram it right out of the back of yo' neck," Toni threatened. "I ain't gon' ask you again. Where is Ice?"

"I-I don't know. He ain't here," Felicia told her in a shaky voice.

"Inside…now!" Toni hissed quietly

Once inside, Toni was accompanied by Milio and his two girls, who were both toting machinery. Milio instructed Sasha to check the small place for others, and Angel to tie up the baby mama to a chair. He was there to make Ice pay for the murder of Mateo, at any cost.

'I'll apologize in advance that you have to be involved in this matter, but I must send a message to Ice," Milio told Felicia in a rather casual manner. He was seated backward in the chair placed before her. "Are you gonna cooperate?"

Felicia said nothing, just glared into his green eyes.

"If you aren't gonna cooperate," Milio went on, "I can have my lovely friend fillet you right now."

Trembling, Felicia said, "What do you want?"

"Not very much at all. Just Ice." Milio handed her her own cell phone and demanded, "Call him. On video."

With the little bit of slack on the rope tied around her and shaky hands, Felicia did as told. "Ice, I love you no matter what happens!" she cried out once Ice appeared on the video call.

"Felicia, hell's goin' on?" Ice wanted to know, not expecting to see his baby mama tied up.

"They got me—"

Ice suddenly witnessed Felicia be backhand slapped and cried out, "Felicia?" He couldn't believe this shit. Reality suddenly seemed as slippery as the narrative of a nightmare.

Toni smirked at Ice and gave him a finger wave over the video call. "Nigga, see what you done got yourself in fuckin' wit' a bitch like me?" she told his ass.

Once Ice saw her, he was brimming with anger. "Bitch, I'ma murk you whenever I catch yo' ass," he threatened.

"Shoulda did that when you came for me. Instead, you got the wrong fuckin' person!" she spat.

"And that person," Milio began as he stepped into frame of the video, "was my kid brother."

"And who the fuck are you?" Ice said to the Spanish guy he'd never seen before.

"I'm the hombre who's gonna make you regret murdering my brother. You've got the next ten minutes. We'll be here awaiting you," Milio told him.

"No, Ice! Don't come!" Felicia shouted in the background before Toni slapped her hard again.

"And if you don't come, then your little lady here will suffer your fate instead." Milio's tone was cold.

Ice refused to turn himself over to them. "You heard her, so don't expect me to come," he stated in a gruff voice. Suddenly it dawned on him that he'd ensured Felicia's death. But he was sure that they would have killed her regardless.

"Then we'll have her alone to die as fast or slow as she wants." Milio spoke without menace in a matter-of-fact tone. He walked over to Felicia, who sat tied up in the chair, with tears running down her cheeks and blood from her mouth. "And I want you to watch every moment of her death," he told Ice. "Toni Montana, show Ice just how much you're cut-throat."

"Say no more."

The gleaming blade transfixed Toni and caused dark images to flicker behind her eyes. She stood behind a helpless Felicia, covering her mouth with her free hand, plunging the knife rapidly deep into Felicia's bulging belly, killing off the unborn child as Felicia squirmed from the sharp pains with muffled screams. Toni then forced Felicia's head tilted back, exposing her throat, and glaring down into Felicia's horrified eyes. She smirked. "Bye, Felicia."

Toni swiftly took the sharp blade across Felicia's throat, slicing it open from ear to ear. As Felicia gasped for air, blood spilled from her throat profusely. A moment later she keeled over, dead.

Ice sat paralyzed while forced to watch the murder of his baby mama and unborn child. Having seen more than enough, he ended the video call with a vow to show no mercy.

***

Jade snorted a line of powdered heroin off the mirror. It stung her nostril and immediately took its course. She'd recently graduated from cocaine, finding the 'ron more effective at numbing her personal pains and making her forget about her problems. It began when she'd came across a pack that was left behind at her place by Banks, and now it had become her new vice. But let her tell it, she was not an addict and could quit whenever she wanted.

There was loud drumming on the front door of her apartment, which awoke Jade as the boy caused her to nod off. She climbed to her feet from the sofa and, in resemblance to a zombie, made her way to the door. After disengaging the lock she pulled the door open, finding Banks. He almost didn't recognize Jade due to her looking sleep-deprived and disheveled and a hot mess. Plus her swollen, discolored eye, courtesy of Gangsta, couldn't go unnoticed. And she was scratching an itch that she couldn't seem to get rid of.

"Look, I'm here to get some shit straight wit'chu," Banks told her forwardly. "Mind if I come in?" Before she could answer, he made his way by her into the unkempt front room. Noticing the dope on the coffee table, Banks shook his head.

Jade closed the door and then turned to Banks, who glared at her, and she said, "Hate that you had to see me like this. Really, I do." She scratched at her neck.

"Jade, since when did you become a fuckin' dopefiend?" he asked in disgust.

"I ain't a dopefiend, a'ight?" she replied, sounding defensive. "I can quit whenever I want. I just been goin' through a lot of shit lately, so when I came across a pack you left behind, I decided to give it a try just to take off the edge."

"But what about your claim of bein' pregnant, Jade? That shit will affect the pregnancy," he told her disapprovingly. And as a second thought, he added, "And how do I even know you're pregnant, when you ain't showin' at all yet?" he observed her skeptically.

Jade looked elsewhere, avoiding him from observing the guilt in her eyes. "So, now you don't believe me?" She tried sounding offended.

"If it makes you feel any better, I still can't believe you had somethin' to do wit' what the fuck happened to Lexi," Banks sniped. "Now answer my damn question."

Jade folded her arms, shifting her weight to one side, and retorted, "I'ont have to answer to you, Banks."

Banks pulled the Glock from his waist, and then held it at his side. "You do and you will. Are you pregnant or not?" he demanded through clenched teeth.

The jig was up. Jade had to own the fact that she wasn't with child. But she feared how Banks might react, remembering it had been the thought of her carrying a baby that spared him from putting a bullet in her damn head before. She could only hope that she could convince him to understand.

"N-no, I'm not," Jade answered in a low, trembling voice.

"So, punk-ass hoe, you been playin' a nigga this entire fuckin time!" Banks was outraged.

"No, I wasn't. I-I-I had a miscarriage. I was gonna tell you eventually, but we haven't talked. You gotta believe me." Jade laid the innocent act on thick.

"Hoe, I'ont believe shit you say," he snarled.

"Jade's sorrowful eyes met Bank's glare, and she pleadingly said, "Banks, I'm sure you hate me, but please don't. I still love you."

Banks scoffed, "You right, I do hate you. Damn, I'ont even know what the fuck I ever saw in you before. Ty was right about everything she said about you fakin' bein' pregnant and bein' a bad friend to Lexi. Only reason I didn't kill yo' ass over Lex before is because you claimed to be pregnant. Well, now it don't matter!"

Banks pressed the muzzle of his Glock to Jade's forehead. He then thought against affording the conniving bitch a fast death. Reluctantly he replaced it on his person.

"You know what? The fuckin' dope will kill you slowly anyway," Banks snarled. He turned for the door and Jade grabbed his arm in attempt to stop him. He snatched it away.

"Yo' ass ain't no better than me, Banks! We're both addicts to the dope just the same! Remember that, Banks!" Jade stepped out of the front door of her apartment, and then she slammed the door shut.

Flopping back down on the sofa, Jade was depressed. She hated the thought of losing Banks, not to mention Gangsta wanted nothing to do with her. On top of that, lately Tywanna had been a thorn in her side, and Jade needed to do something about her.

Needing to clear her head space, Jade leaned in to do another line, catching her own reflection in the mirror the dope was laid out on. It was like she didn't recognize the girl staring back at her, who looked terrible. She just closed her eyes and snorted the heroin.

Banks climbed into his Aston, which was parked before Jade's apartment complex. Resting his head back against the headrest, he let out a deep breath. He watched the snow fall lazily from the black sky. Seeing Jade had brought back so many memories for him, good and bad. He thought about Lexi and the love he held for her. What he wouldn't give to have her back.

His mind shifted to Jade, how he went from having feelings for her to despising her. She had caused him more pain than anyone. Although he hated to see her victim to the dope, he wondered if it was any truth to her stating they're both adducts to the dope equally in their own ways. This slid his thoughts to his mother falling victim to dope. His eyes became misty thinking about losing her. Banks was hurt from losing women he dearly cared about. Beginning with Tywanna, he vowed not to let it happen again.

Banks started his Aston and pulled off, driving through the thin white veil of snow, nodding his head to the sounds of 21-Savage's "A lot".

***

Scarface was displaying on mute on the large projector screen in the theater room of the safehouse. Diamond and Toni were seated before the screen. They were meeting in order to discuss their street affairs.

"See, he knows what it takes to be in power," Toni commented, referring to the iconic character, the Cuban gangster Tony Montana.

"Toni, power is a wonderful thing. But if you ain't enough without it, you won't be enough wit' it," Diamond expressed. He took a swig from his glass of Remy. "You know, I can't apologize enough for how things were between us."

"Likewise."

"Didn't want things to be that way, but you know how the games goes."

"And I respect the game, Diamond," she told him. She planted her hand on top of his free hand in his lap. "That's all behind us, and now things can go back to the way it was before everything went wrong." Her tone was hopeful.

"'Fraid not, after all of the damage done not only on our behalves, but Gangsta's gone rogue and Chase is dead."

"Unfortunately, there's nothin' we can do to bring back Chase. But maybe we can convince Gangsta to partner with us again. And if anyone can do it, it's you," she suggested.

Diamond shook his head. "Gangsta will never agree to that. He's too damn determined to prove to me that he doesn't need me. Even if that means either him or me havin' to kill or be killed," he expounded. Although he wondered why Gangsta spared him the night at the club, perhaps it was the same reason he'd been sparing Gangsta.

"I know the feelin' all too well," Toni responded ruefully.

"I'm sure." Diamond sipped at his drink. "Must say, I never doubted that you could head yo' own gang under me. It wasn't about me choosin' Major over you. I just' wanted to keep you close to me as possible," he felt the need to explain.

"Diamond, you taught me almost everything I know in the streets, so trust, I can handle my own."

"And look at you now, the Trap Queen. In charge of yo' own operation. But tell me, what about yo' connect? If we're gonna join forces, then there should only be one connect between us, and I prefer it be Balistrieri," Diamond proposed.

Toni leaned back in her seat. "I have no problem with that, but only on one condition: I conduct business with Balistrieri personally."

"Done," he agreed.

"Besides, I have never actually had a connect," she told him.

"Then how you supply yo' operation?"

"Mateo's brother happens to be a kingpin down in Miami. Mateo introduced me to him when I was in need of product, and he and I made an arrangement— a favor for a favor," Toni explained. "He had flown here to take care of our final business before returnin' to Miami with Mateo's body for proper burial. I won't be seein' much of him now that Mateo's gone." Heartache could be detected in her words.

"Here, this'll take some of the edge off." Diamond handed her the remains of his glass of Remy, and she drained it. "Look, I'm sure Mateo meant a lot to you. But wit' all due respect, I'm grateful it wasn't you," he said in a meaningful tone of voice.

Diamond saw Toni eyeing him speculatively. He met her gaze squarely, and they looked into each other's eyes. Diamond licked his lips, feeling himself fill with lust just looking at her, wanting more than anything to wrap his arms around her and hold her tight. He reached out and brushed some of her long locks away from her face in order to see just how beautiful she was. Toni took hold of his hand in both her and pulled it close to her, wanting Diamond to know she was there for him. Diamond began to pull Toni in for a kiss, and she didn't resist as their lips grew inches apart.

"Diamond, you in here?" Major called out as he stepped into the theater room. His untimely interruption caused Diamond and Toni to pull back, but not before Major saw them.

Diamond hurried to his feet. "Yeah, I'm here."

"Didn't say shit about her bein' here when you called me over," Major commented in a flat tone as he stepped up.

"Actually, Toni's the reason why I called you over. She and I talked it out and got past our problems. And you should know that she'll be partnerin' wit' us," Diamond informed him.

Major's brows furrowed. "So what, we're jus' s'posed to get past the fact that she brought the rat nigga Pelle around, who almost got all of us indicted?" he fumed.

Toni jumped to her feet in her Prada heels. "Look, I can't take back that I misjudged Pelle, okay. But I smoked his ass to right my wrong, which is why none of us have to worry about a damn indictment. Don't I deserve respect for that, Major?" she raved.

"Maybe yo' ass has somethin' to do wit' how shit went down," Major sniped.

"Nigga, are you accusin' me of workin' with the fuckin' Feds?" Toni snarled.

"Possible," he snorted.

Toni stole on Major, putting blood in his mouth. "You got me fucked up!" She was outraged.

"Bitch, I should beat yo' ass," Major growled.

"Try me," she dared, jamming a finer in his face.

Diamond intervened. "Both of you, enough," he demanded of them. "Toni, why don't you go grab yo'self a drink while I talk wit' Major a moment."

Toni sharply eyed Major before she made her way for the wet bar located in the dining room. And Major glared at Toni her entire way out of the theater room. Diamond knew he had to be the one to get Toni and Major to see eye to eye.

Turning his attention to Major, Diamond said, "Listen, I get your concern. But despite the misjudgment she made of Pelle, I trust Toni."

"If you say so," Major replied, shaking his head. It appeared to him there was something more than what Diamond was leading on.

"And you know how much I trust you wit' my life. So whatever beef you two have needs to be ended."

"Look, I have nothin' personal against Toni. But why should she be allowed back at the table?"

"Though you'd be smart enough to recognize why, Major. Now that Toni has her own franchise, wit' her as a partner, we stand to move much more product and can even expand our drug distribution throughout the state. Not to mention added firepower for war in the streets," Diamond explained, and Major had to admit he made a point.

"A'ight," Major concurred. "Jus' make sure you keep her ass under control." He used his backhand to wipe away blood from the corner of his mouth.

Returning to the theater room, Toni had a bottle of Remy in hand. Without a word to either of the boys, she retook her seat before the projector screen and watched the film. She hit the bottle.

"Toni, listen——"

Holding up a hand, Major cut Diamond short. Then Major turned to Toni and told her, "Believe it or not, I think it's a good idea to partner wit' you. And for the record, I respect yo' gangsta, Toni."

"We good, Major. A bitch done messed up her manicure fuckin' wit'chu," Toni chuckled.

"Now, let's run the game." Diamond told them.

"Ooh, this my favorite part!" Toni said excitedly, referring to the iconic scene of Tony Montana fearlessly letting his submachine gun rip on his enemies. She imitated Tony Montana: "Say 'ello to my little friend!"

Diamond and Major just looked at one another, shaking their heads.

Troublesome

Chapter 17

Fuck Jade; fuck Banks; fuck Diamond; fuck Yul; Fuck 'em all! Gangsta raved introspectively. He was lounging on the sofa in the front room of his loft. Most of the overhead lights were off. The crescent moon painted everything on the other side of the windows with stark, eerie light, fitting his mood. Gangsta was on a coke binge. He hadn't been out of the crib in days since airing out Magic Clippers. And he'd gotten word that Banks managed to survive the brazen attack. Gangsta was still healing from the bullet he took from Banks, and he wanted Banks to feel his pain. He needed a moment away from all of the drama, although it was all in his mind.

Can't believe I let Jade's hoe ass play me, Gangsta seethed. Whole time the hoe been fuckin' and suckin' Banks behind my back. And I got some hot shit for Banks's ass. Nigga gon' regret not finishin' me. Talkin' 'bout he wouldn't have done the shit if it wasn't for Diamond. Shit, if it wasn't for me sparin' Diamond, then Diamond would be the one finished. He shook his head.

When Gangsta was about to off Diamond the night at Red Velvet, he never expected that Banks would ambush them. And he didn't want to admit that he spared Diamond from Banks's bullets, taking one himself, because part of him still had love for Diamond. And if anyone was gonna smoke Diamond it was gonna be him - after he smoked Banks.

As much as I hate to admit it, Diamond was right about Yul, Gangsta reflected. And now I gotta get him before he get me. Once I get rid of him and the rest, then I'ma lockdown these streets. And ain't no one gon' stop me.

A rap on the front door pulled Gangsta from his inner thoughts. He figured it must be Ashley at the door, since she texted him earlier that she'd be drooping by. He knew she wanted to talk with him about what happened with Lexi, and he hoped that by telling her the truth, she would forgive him. He understood how painful it was to lose a close friend because he felt it behind losing Chase. Gangsta only wanted for him and Ash to continue to be close, after all.

Just to be on the safe side, Gangsta grabbed the Draco off the end table, and then slunk to the door. "Who dat?" he called out.

"Open up, G. It's Playboy," came from the other side.

Gangsta unbolted the locks, and then pulled open the door for his right-hand man.

Stepping inside the loft, Playboy immediately observed the place was mostly lit by moonlight spilling in through the windows, and both Gangsta and his crib were unkempt. *Dis nigga losin' it*, Playboy told himself introspectively.

"Ain't expect you to drop by,' Gangsta said as he locked the door.

"Been hittin' you up for days tryin' to get in touch. No answer," Playboy replied.

"Been layin' low," he responded as he turned for the front room with Playboy in tow.

"Damn, homie, what's wit' the gun?" Playboy asked, noticing the Draco in Gangsta's hands.

Gangsta stepped behind the wet bar and set the weapon on the bar top and stated, "I'm jus' stayin' ready to go out bustin', nah'mean?"

"Yeah. Know exactly what you mean," Playboy remarked, brimming with grief. He took a seat on the sofa. "Well, while you been layin' low, the operation has been sinkin', and niggas are beginnin' to jump ship because we don't have enough work to supply the entire crew."

"Look, I'm workin' on it, A'ight?" Annoyed, Gangsta grabbed a squat glass and then pulled down a bottle of Patron. The light fixture illuminating the shelves of the bottles casted light across the front room, Gangsta poured himself a generous amount of the tequila and took a swig.

"Gangsta, you shoulda reconsidered cuttin' off Yul. He was frontin' us wit' all the work we needed," Playboy put out there.

"And that same work was bringin' heat from Twelve to our operations due to so many cases of OD's. Cuttin' the shit wit' fentanyl was bad for business," Gangsta objected.

"At least we were makin' profit. Now we're barely makin' any."

"Listen, we don't need Yul or his fuckin' product to make money. Besides, I'ma off his ass anyway," he hissed.

"That's the problem. You wanna off Yul when he's our best chance at takin' shit over. Can't let you do that, G," Playboy told him disapprovingly. He stood and whipped a Glock .9 off his waist, then leveled it in Gangsta.

"Yul sent you, huh?" Gangsta scoffed and shook his head. He tossed back the remains of his drink and then set the glass in the bar top with a thud beside the Draco.

"Wanted to tell you that Yul came to me wit' a proposition. Now you know."

"And you know I stay ready," Gangsta stated.

In a motion almost too fast to follow, he grabbed up the Draco, aiming at Playboy, and the two matched guns.

Pop-Pop!

Boc-boc-boc!

The two simultaneously busted at one another, Gangsta's bullets wildly missed, tearing holes in the wall, as Playboy's tore holes in his chest. On impact, the bullets forced Gangsta backward crashing into the shelved mounted on the wall, which caused glassware and liquor bottles to fall onto the floor. He ended up slumped back up against the wall chasing his breath. Playboy stepped around the bar and put his foot in a puddle of liquor, standing over Gangsta and aiming down on his bald head.

"This isn't about betrayal," Playboy said to hip.

Pop!

Leaving Gangsta for dead, Playboy strolled out of the loft. But unbeknownst to him, however, Gangsta had a few more breaths, and he mustered up enough strength to poorly fingerpaint the initials "PB" in his own blood on the wall. Before taking his final breath, Gangsta was sure Playboy's death was written in blood.

After leaving Gangsta for dead, Playboy made his way to the warehouse in order to see Yul. Escorted by an armed dread-head, he was taken to the back room, where the Mega Don Yul was awaiting, and Siah and Rasheym were present also. Yul was seated at a small table cleaning his Desert Eagle handgun, shells scattered atop the table.

"Me take it you hav' somedin' you wan' tell me since you here," Yul assumed. He didn't brother to look up from his task of cleaning the weapon, which Playboy remembered Yul shooting him with all too well during their first time ever meeting.

"It's done," Playboy told him, and Yul understood.

Giving Playboy his undivided attention, Yul eyed him and remarked, "Irie. Me knew you had it in you, mon."

"I did my part; now you do yours."

"No worries. Me will wipe out Diamond an' his connect soon enough," he assured him.

"I'll lay low until then." Playboy turned and made his way out, escorted by the armed dread-head.

Now that Gangsta was disposed of, Yul planned to use Playboy instead to move his product. First he had to get rid of Diamond and Frank Balistrieri in order to have a significant role on the drug trade. And to do so, he was more than willing to shower bullets on them.

After loading the Desert Eagle, Yul cocked its slide. He looked to Siah and Rasheym and stated, "Everybody must dead."

***

The Rolls Royce came to a halt yards apart from the Jeep Wrangler in the boat yard, where all sorts of expensive boats were stored. Frank had come there to have a meet with Yul. The request had been made by Yul, and Frank decided on the location. Both of the crime lords were there not knowing what to expect of the other, although neither was intimidated.

Little and Alphonse debarked from the Rolls. Alphonse pulled open the rear suicide door for Frank. Rasheym and Siah stood with weapons in hand near the Jeep, on either side of Yul. Leaving their men behind, the Italian Mob boss and Jamaican Mega Don approached one another. The two crime lords stared at each other, taking each other's measures,

"Here we are," Frank began in an even tone. "How about we cut to the chase?"

"Fine wit' me," Yul concurred. "Me aware dat you hav' control over a great deal of de drug trade in de streets. An' me wan' offer to purchase a portion of you territory for me own operation."

"And why should I sell you a portion of my territory when I stand to make more money than you'll ever be able to offer?"

"Not only will me posse continue to distribute some of you product as consolation, but we no hav' to go to war over money," Yul added in an even tone, watching Frank's face to measure the impact of his threat.

Frank maintained a face of stone. "I must decline your offer." He turned aside as though to leave, then had a last thought. "A war is inevitable over power or money." With no further words, Frank turned on his way to the Rolls.

Yul was sure Frank would decline his offer. In fact, he'd only requested to meet with Frank just to draw him in. With a gesture of the hand, Yul summoned his Rastas, who'd been patient, but ready to dump.

Rrraa-rrraaa-rrraaa!

Boc, boc, boc, boc!

Rasheym and Siah opened fire on the Italians, and instantaneously, Little and Alphonse fired back at the Jamaicans. In the midst of the exchange of fire, Frank and Yul drew their own weapons, and then took part. Gunfire echoed inside the boat yard as shells from each gang tinkled on the pavement. Two slugs landed in Alphonse's stomach, putting him down, and as Frank helped him to his feet, Little covered them. A bullet to the thigh stumbled Siah, while Yul and Rasheym continued letting off.

Frank helped a profusely bleeding Alphonse into the rear seat of the Rolls, and Little hurried inside behind the wheel. As the Rolls peeled away in reverse of the boat yard, bullets bounced off of its bulletproof exterior. Turning for the Jeep, Yul discovered one of its front tires flattened from a stray bullet, preventing them from being able to give chase.

With the Mafia and the Shower Posse now at war, it wouldn't end until either Frank or Yul were taken out.

**

Pacing back and forth in the study of his mansion, Frank was infuriated. His white Tom Ford button down, which he had untucked and rolled up at the sleeve, was stained crimson from the blood of Alphonse. As they had fled the boat yard with Frank cradling Alphonse in his arms, unfortunately he passed away from the fatal shots he suffered. And losing one of his closet comrades deeply affected Frank.

Seated back on the Italian leather sofa, Diamond observed the Mob boss. Subsequent to their great escape, Frank had summoned him. Diamond had never witnessed Frank so furious. He knew Frank was out to get even.

"I want those fuckin' islanders offed!" Frank raged. "Where in the hell do they get off tryin' to take over? Well, over my dead body!"

"Are you a'ight, Mr. Balistrieri?" Diamond asked.

Frank took a seat beside him. "It's tough on me losing Al. He was like a nephew to me. Dammit, I hate to have to call Al's mother with the news." He let out a deep breath.

Little approached with a glass of scotch in one hand and its bottle in the other. "Boss, maybe you should have yourself a drink." He offered the glass.

Instead, Frank grabbed the bottle from him, and then turned it up to his lips. Just as much as Frank, Little was pained by the death of Alphonse also. Before taking a drink, he raised the glass. "To Alphonse."

"I just don't get it. Why all of a sudden would those damn slinky-heads come for me?" Frank questioned no one in particular.

"That sleazy Agent Lynch may have sent 'em," Little suggested.

"No, I'm sure Lunch had nothin' to do wit' it," Diamond chimed in.

"And how do you figure that, kid, after all the things he's done?" Frank inquired.

"'Cause the leader of the Jamaicans, Yul, isn't the type to take orders from Lynch, or anyone. I'm sure it's jus' Yul's attempt at a rise to power."

"What makes you so sure about this?" Frank wanted to know.

Diamond rested his forearms on his knees. "A while back, Yul approached me wit' an offer to supply me, and I declined, tellin' him that I already had a connect. Apparently he's planned to take you out ever since, so I'd need his supply."

"Thought we agreed that me being your connect's on a need-to-know basis, Diamond," he retorted.

"And it is. More than likely Gangsta told him when he decided to betray me and take Yul's offer behind my back," Diamond explained.

"Then let's go have a talk with Gangsta," Little insisted. "Make sure he never talk again."

Diamond quickly said, "No, I'll talk wit' Gangsta. Alone." Instead, like Toni suggested, he'd first try to convince Gangsta to side wit' them. But if not, then he'd rather whack Gangsta himself. Only he was too late and didn't know.

Frank planted a hand on Diamond's shoulder and stated, "Sounds to me like you've been owing him this talk for betraying you. Well, dead men can't betray."

Troublesome

Chapter 18

Following Gangsta's dismal funeral ceremony, Diamond and others carried his casket from the church, then placed it inside an awaiting hearse.

Diamond mourned Gangsta, but with a greater passion, he hated that Gangsta had been afforded no dignity by his murderer. Gangsta had betrayed Diamond, but that didn't matter anymore. On the edge of the dark, on the brink of the void, few offenses were worth remembering. The only things worth recalling were the moments of friendship and laughter. If they had been at odds on Gangsta's last day, they were on the same team now, with the same singular adversary.

Needing a moment to gather himself, Diamond took a seat on the church's steps. He looked up into the brilliant sun. It was odd, still cold enough to see his breath with the sun so bright overhead. The bright sun had melted most of the ice and was pockmarking the snow, leaving slush wherever humans drove and walk.

Toni and Major also sat on the steps on either side of Diamond.

"Are you okay, Diamond?" Toni asked, sympathetic.

Diamond deeply exhaled, breath frosting the air, "I still can't believe this shit happened to Gangsta."

"We gotta do somethin' about this," Major insisted.

"And we will," Diamond swore.

"First we need to figure out who murked Gangsta," Toni said.

"Ashley mentioned noticin' the letters PB scribbled in blood on the wall near where she found his body," Major mentioned.

"Gangsta was tryin' to let it be known who killed him," Diamond figured. "And for someone to catch him slackin' in his own crib means he never saw it comin'. Had to be someone Gangsta trusted," he said thoughtfully.

"Like one of his boys," Toni added.

Major put two and two together, jumped to his feet, and then said, "I know who killed Gangsta."

"Who the hell is it?" Diamond eagerly wanted to know. He stood, and Toni followed.

"Playboy," he unveiled. "Nigga was Gangsta's right hand-man, and if anyone could have gotten close to Gangsta wit'out bein' suspected, it's him."

"Makes sense. But why in the hell would Playboy do Gangsta?" Toni wondered.

"That's somethin' we're gonna have to make Playboy tell us himself," Diamond stated.

"And I know where we can find his ass," Toni told them.

"Where is he?" Diamond asked eagerly.

"I'll tell you on the way."

Before heading for the vehicle, the trio offered Ashley their condolences once again. Witnessing her so hurt behind her brother's murder was particularly difficult for Diamond, since he had planned to murder Gangsta himself, if need be. However, he wasn't willing to accept that someone else did.

Diamond turned Tywanna and told her, "Love, I want you to look after Ash. I gotta go."

"You're about to go after whoever killed Gangsta, aren't you, Diamond?" Ty's question was more of a statement. Deep down inside, she hoped it wasn't Banks.

Diamond looked away, seeing Tori and Major entering his Porsche truck. "Can't let this go unanswered, Ty," he said in a low voice.

"I don't want you to go. What if somethin' also happens to you, then what am I supposed to do?" Her voice cracked and tears rimmed her eyes. "I can't continue livin' in fear of you endin' up back in jail or dead. Diamond, you need to get outta the damn game before it's too late," she cried.

Diamond didn't want to tell Tywanna right then and there that he did plan to retire from the game eventually, because he didn't know exactly when that would be. And he didn't want for her to be expecting it to be sooner than he was able.

"Listen," Diamond began evenly. "Don't worry about me right now. I'll be back before you know it." He pecked Ty on her lips before heading to the Porsche.

The trio rose in a moment's silence as if on behalf of Gangsta. They each had their own respective reason for grieving his death. And they each collectively wanted vengeance.

While steering the Porsche, Diamond glanced over at Toni, and asked, "Now, where the hell can we find Playboy?"

"The Comfort Suites," she answered.

Pulling up the hotel on his GPS, Diamond headed in that direction.

"Toni, how do you know where to find this nigga?" Major inquired from the rear seat.

"Seen him out with Gangsta once, and the nigga tried to kick some corny-ass game to me. And when I turned him down he thought it was a good idea to tell me where his usual spot is, wishin' for me to show up," she explained.

"Then he should be careful what he wishes for," Diamond said. He pulled to a stop at a red light.

Boom!

Suddenly the rear of the Porsche truck imploded from a shotgun blast. Luckily, none of the three was hit. They looked back, finding a gunman hanging partway out from a Jeep. None of them noticed they were being tailed.

Grabbing their cannons, the trio jumped out of the Porsche, exchanging shots with the assailants that were five deep. Diamond left off his twin .45s rapidly, Toni unleashed her Mini-14 while sawing it side to side, and Major opened up his Glock .27 with his palm over his forearm so he could shoot straight. During the gunfight, the trio gunned down the assailants. Except one, who fled into the Jeep, and then recklessly peeled away. Noticing one of the remaining assailants on the pavement, breathing raggedly and grabbing for his weapon, Diamond stepped over him. He recognized the assassin as of the Rastas he had saw with Yul. It was Siah. Before allowing him to grab the weapon, Diamond targeted his already bullet-wounded chest.

Boc, boc, boc!

Back in the Porsche, speeding away, sirens wailed in the distance.

"Fuck them niggas come from?" Major asked no one in particular, looking around for any more tails.

"More importantly: who sent 'em?" Toni added.

"Yul sent 'em. I recognized one of his Rastas," Diamond told them. He dipped around the vehicle.

"But why would Yul send shooters at us?" she inquired.

"Sure it has somethin' to do with' Gangsta, since he was dealin' wit' Yul," Major said.

"Only thing is, Gangsta said that their business was done, and that Yul wants me dead. Not to mention Yul also went after Balistrieri," Diamond expounded. "I get the feelin' this shit wit' Yul has to do wit' Playboy."

They headed for the Comfort Suites, the GPS guiding their way.

***

For the past week, Playboy had been holed up in the Comfort Suites. To keep his mind off of shit, he'd been spending the days constantly intoxicated and smashing different thots, although it wasn't enough to relieve the flashes of smoking Gangsta crossing his mind. He was aware that today was the day of Gangsta's funeral, which he was sure Diamond would attend. And Playboy was expecting Yul to take out Diamond and his connect, then together, he and the Jamaican drug boss could take over the game. But unbeknownst to him, both Diamond and his connect had proven to be difficult to take out.

After smashing the thot in his company, Playboy lay numb on the bed. "Damn, Kat, that shit was bomb," he praised. As she rolled out of the bed, he asked, "Where yo' ass goin'?"

Kat pulled his tank top over her head and then said, "Chill, daddy. I'm just goin' to the bathroom."

"Don't take long, 'cause a nigga can't wait for some more of that bomb pussy."

As she strolled out of the room Playboy observed her ass bounce. He sat back up against the headboard, pulled out a cigarette from the pack of Newports on the bedside table, and then lit it. His iPhone rang. He reached over, grabbing the phone, and answered. "Yeah." He puffed the cigarette.

"Us missed dem," the caller told him. It was Yul.

Playboy jumped out of bed. "Thought you had shit under control!" he cried out.

"No worries. Us will get dem." Click.

"Shit." Playboy was frustrated, hurling his phone against the wall, smashing it to pieces. He flounced down on the edge of the bed and pulled on the square. With Diamond still alive, Playboy knew his ploy to take over the game was in jeopardy. If need be would off Diamond himself...

Hearing Kat shriek broke Playboy's thoughts. He jumped to his feet and grabbed the Glock with the thirty-shot clip off the nightstand, then aimed it toward the ajar door. Someone was there for him, his thoughts registered quickly. Suddenly the door came crashing open and he squeezed.

Blam, blam, blam, blam!

Playboy filled Kat with shots. She had been forcefully shoved through the door into the bedroom to surprise him. Her dead frame fell into Playboy, causing him to drop his gun. Diamond followed by Toni and Major came charging into the room with their guns on Playboy.

Unknotting his black Versace tie, Diamond tossed it at Playboy and then demanded, "Tie it around your neck."

In the nude, Playboy's hands had been bound behind his back, and he struggled to keep his balance on his tiptoes while standing on a chair. Diamond's tie was strung up to an overhead light fixture and made into a noose. Playboy knew his life was only hanging on by a thread.

"Why'd you kill Gangsta?" Diamond demanded. He, flanked by Toni and Major, stood before Playboy.

"I-I had no choice," Playboy stammered.

"How come you had no choice?" he pressed.

"It-it was Yul. He threatened to kill my family if I didn't kill Gangsta. Came to me behind Gangsta's back, upset that Gangsta stopped dealin' wit' him."

"And I'm sure Yul offered to replace Gangsta wit' you, right?" Diamond's question was more of a statement.

Playboy ruefully nodded. "Like I said, I had no choice." He swallowed hard.

"You coulda told Gangsta so he could take out Yul. Instead, you chose to allow greed make you betray Gangsta!" Diamond boomed.

"Don't you get it? Whether I killed him or not, regardless, Yul was gonna kill Gangsta. Yul's the one you want. You can't hang this one on me!" Playboy cried out pleadingly.

Diamond glared at him. "Or can I?"

He kicked the chair from beneath Playboy's feet, causing the noose to tighten around his neck as he hung. Diamond, along with Tori and Major, observed as Playboy helplessly squirmed. Each squirm elicited some further gasp from Playboy, his eyes and tongue protruding in an ugly manner. A moment later, Playboy's body hung lifeless.

Everything Diamond had gathered from Playboy solidified his assumptions of Yul. One thing for sure: Diamond would make Yul pay with death.

***

"Me wan' Diamond dead tonight!" Yul raged. "Go Rastas, an' let no mon steer from de path me hav' made. Dem streets out dere belongs to you now!"

After fleeing the gunfight with Diamond and the others, Rasheym had immediately reported to Yul at the warehouse. Not only was Yul outraged about Diamond managing to evade the ambush, but also that Siah was left dead in the act. Before either Diamond or Frank Balistrieri could retaliate, Yul wanted them both eliminated.

Rasheym assembled numerous heavily-armed Rastas. While gathered outside in front of the building, Rasheym was giving the other Rastas orders. He noticed the Rolls Royce accelerating up the street towards them, and immediately Rasheym opened up on the vehicle with his M-16.

Rrraaa-rrraaa-rrraaa!

Bullets ricocheted off the exterior of the bulletproof Rolls, shielding everyone inside. Little was behind the wheel while Diamond rode shotgun and Toni and Major took the rear. They were there to wipeout the Shower Posse once and for all. And Diamond wanted nothing more than to be sure to get revenge on Yul.

The Rasta continued showering bullets on the Rolls. Rasheym rushed inside the building to warn Yul of the attack. Once Little yielded the Rolls before the building, Diamond and Major hurried out, and Toni rose from its sunroof. Each of the three traded shots with the Rastas. During the course of the shootout, Little was able to make it to the trunk and he pulled out an M-72 L.A.W. Rocket, balancing the weapon of mass destruction on his shoulder, and then launched a missile at the warehouse.

Upon impact, the missile exploded, blowing a crater in the building. Yul felt himself thrown backward from the terrible explosion. Almost before he realized what was happening, he crashed onto the floor, knocking all the breath out of his body. Yul writhed on the floor, trying desperately to get his breath. He drew air into his lings and savored it. He grunted deeply and resolved to kill Diamond. Another explosion like that one, whatever it was, might kill him next time.

The money! Yul's conscience considered. He shot to his feet, discovering the place in bad shape from the blast. The lights flickered, and flames and smoke had set off the water sprinklers. Yul desperately wanted to save the money stored inside the safe. He hurried to safe, placing his green eye to its retinal scan, and disengaged the locks. He began transferring stacks of cash from the safe into a duffel bag in order to take with him as much of the money as he could carry. Hearing a shootout erupt nearby inside of the warehouse, Yul quickly registered someone was definitely there trying to kill him. He shut the safe and pulled the Desert Eagle as the gunman stepped into the room armed with two guns. It was none other Diamond.

"Ah, Diamond, me knew you would come for me eventually," Yul told him. They held each other at gunpoint.

"Couldn't let you get away after all you've done, Yul," Diamond stated. Their eyes were locked.

"Me do whateva me hav' to do."

"Then do or die!"

"Boc, boc, boc, boc!

Shots were exchanged between them. Diamond took cover behind a brick pillar while Yul ducked beside the safe. As they traded fire, bullets knocked chunks out of the pillar and bounced off the safe, neither able to get a good shot. In between the fire and smoke, the two needed to get out of the building soon, but not before one of them killed the other. During the shootout, Diamond managed to hit Yul in the shoulder, causing Yul to drop his weapon.

Diamond began approaching Yul with intentions to smoke him, then suddenly Rasheym barged through the room's side door, bustin' his M-16 at Diamond, who instantly took cover behind the pillars as rounds just missed him.

Rasheym had been out back awaiting in the Jeep for Yul to make a getaway when the explosion took place. And, fortunately for Yul, he didn't hesitate to enter the partly destroyed, burning building to be sure the Mega Don was still in one piece. If not, then Yul would have been at Diamond's mercy.

While Diamond was held pinned behind the pillar by Rasheym's rapid gunfire, Yul hurried out the side door and Rasheym backed his way out also. Immediately, Diamond went after them, finding that the door led into a corridor that had access to the rear exit of the building. Filling the corridor with bullets behind Yul and Rasheym, Diamond just barely missed them as they scrambled out of the exit. As Diamond began to make his way out of the exit also, a spray of bullets forced him to duck back inside. A moment later, Diamond barged out of the building just as Yul and

Rasheym were peeling away. He filled the Jeep with bullets as it sped off.

Diamond was furious that Yul managed to escape death, but now Yul knew he was out for blood. And Yul was livid that he had to leave behind the safe full of money because of Diamond. Somehow, he had to make Diamond pay.

The two were bound to meet again, and the only option would be death, because neither could live while the other survived.

Troublesome

Chapter 19

"I'd like to thank all of you for comin' out to show ya boy love and support. And a special thanks to those who believed in me and my dream. Wit'out you, this record deal wouldn't be possible. Now here's the premiere to my new music video for the single 'Money Shower'. Enjoy."

Tonight Major's album release party was being held at Red Velvet, and everyone who was someone came out to support him, including Gucci Mane. Major had signed a development deal with So Icey entertainment, and suddenly everyone wanted a piece of Major. His name had vastly blown up in the rap game with "Money Shower" being a hit and its music video going viral. Now more than ever, Major's dream was coming true.

Making his way off the main stage after his announcement, Major approached Diamond, who was seated at the bar in the VIP lounge. He took up the stool beside Diamond and said, "'Preciate you puttin' together this party for me."

"You deserve it, my nigga. I'm proud of you," Diamond expressed. He took a drink from his glass of Henny. "Besides, it's the least I could do for you after all you've done for me," he added.

"Diamond, I did those things outta my loyalty for you, so don't mention it," Major told him. "Look, I'll get wit' you in a minute. I need to go holla at the homie Gucci Mane." He dapped up Diamond before heading towards the table occupied by Gucci Mane and his entourage.

Diamond decided to go over and check on the girls, Tywanna, Toni, and Ashley, who were seated on a red velvet sofa in the lounge. The party of three had been enjoying each other's company, not to mention bottle service.

"Are you all enjoyin' the night?" asked Diamond of the girls.

"Don't get me wrong, it's lit in here and all, but I'm really ready to go home, Diamond," Ty told him. She rose to her feet in Balenciaga sling backs and whispered something provocative into his ear.

Diamond peeped at his Breitling Timepiece. "Jus' gimme an hour, then I'll take you home."

"Diamond, you stay," Toni chimed in. She stood. "I'll take her home."

"I'd appreciate it," he said.

"Anything for you, Diamond. Besides, I ran outta singles makin' it rain on the strippers." She smirked.

"And you can drop me off along the way, I should get home to the twins," Ash piped in. "Just gimme a sec to let Major know I'll be leavin'. I'm sure he'll wanna stay and continue to celebrate." She polished off her glass of Rosé before stepping away to go see Major.

Ty wrapped her arms around Diamonds neck and seductively said, "I'ma be waitin' up for you." She kissed him.

"And I won't keep you waitin' long," Diamond promised, looking into her eyes with fondness.

"How 'bout y'all share the love," Toni half-joked.

"You know we love you, Toni." Ty chuckled.

Ash returned with Major. The girls all congratulated him on his album release once again. Afterwards, they bounced.

"Too bad the girls decided to bounce," Major said. He tossed an arm around Diamond's shoulders. "But after all the shit we done been through, and all of the niggas we had to tend to, we earned the right to enjoy the rest of this night." He poured the battle of Ace of Space to his lips.

"Can't agree more." Diamond grinned.

The two occupied a table near the main stage. The club's lights were down low while Mahogany performed to "Money Shower." She also was a vixen in its music video, propelling it to go viral online with her exclusive dance moves. On stage, Mahogany was positioned in a standing split while making her ass cheeks clap. Cast crowded the stage, makin' it rain on her, including Gucci Mane. She only wore a black lace bra and G-string with yellow Manolo pumps, and her performance was sensational.

Diamond took a swig from his glass of Henny. "Shit won't be the same wit'out you around here, Major," he stressed.

"I won't be like all those studio gangstas who makes it big and then forgets where he comes from. I'll always do what I have to," Major responded.

Diamond shifted towards him and said, "I'ont want you doin' anything else that doesn't have to do wit' yo' rap career. I mean it, Major."

"And what about you? I mean, I'ont want you to end up goin' like Gangsta did, Diamond," There was a hint of concern in Major's tone.

"Yeah, I know what you mean. I hate how Gangsta went out." He sipped at his drink.

"Let's face it, Diamond, there's no future in the game. Sooner or later someone will catch up to you. The plan was to get rich, not die," Major stressed.

"Listen, I'll be gettin' out the game soon enough. Already told Balistrieri he'll be in need of a replacement."

"Then maybe you'll move out to ATL wit' me," Major suggested.

"I have other plans in mind. But I'm sure you and Ash will love it there."

"Ash won't be comin'," Major replied, sounding a bit disappointed.

"And why not?"

"Said I should go alone to focus on my career and get myself established, then we'll figure it out."

"Sounds to me like Ash jus' wanna see you succeed. Believe me, she's good for you."

"I could say the same for Ty when it comes to you. But I get the feelin' there's more to yo' bond wit' Toni," Major told him.

Diamond looked to him and said, "Toni and I just' have deep bond. Nothin' more, nothin' less."

"All I'm sayin' is watch out for a dilemma," he said, giving Diamond something to reflect on. "But do you."

"Fa sho'."

"Cool. Now how 'bout we join in on the fun." Major approached the stage with a fistful of singles and showered Mahogany with money.

***

After Ashley had been dropped off, once arriving at the condo complex, Tywanna invited Toni inside to keep her company. The two had their heels kicked off while chillin' on the love seat, listening to the sounds of Lizzo on Alexa, and smoking a blunt of kush.

Ty puffed the blunt. "Toni, I'm glad that you and Diamond were able to salvage your bond," she said.

"And he and I wouldna been able to if it wasn't for you,' Toni said thankfully. "Lemme ask you somethin': what makes you love Diamond as much as you do?" she wanted to know.

"Where do I begin?" Ty commented, reflecting on everything she loved about Diamond. She puffed the blunt before passing it to Toni. "Well, the most compellin' thing about Diamond is he's emotional. Although his emotions and the ability to really feel is never a contradiction to his edge. To answer your question, I love Diamond so much because he knows how to love," she expressed. Then she added, "And did I mention he's fine with a big dick." Ty grinned.

"Aaoow!" Toni exclaimed, mimicking Cardi B, and high-fived Ty. "Seriously though, Ty, it's no doubt that you and Diamond love each other for all the right reasons." She understood exactly why Ty loved Diamond.

"Diamond obviously really has a lot of love for you, Toni. I see it whenever you're together."

"Of course, girl, me and his big-head ass been close since we were young. But you're the only one who offered him everything he wants in a woman."

Ty hung her head and quietly replied, "Everything except maybe a child." Her words weighed on Toni.

"Ty," Toni began tenderly, "you deserve to have a child with Diamond. Although it's apparent he loves you regardless." She gentle rubbed Ty's arm, comforting her.

"I'm sure you're right, Toni. Thanks for your comfort," Ty said sincerely.

"I got'chu, girl." Toni took a pull of the blunt, then passed it to Ty and said, "That'll comfort you even more." She smiled. Toni genuinely cared about Tywanna as a friend, and knew the feeling was mutual.

In that moment, Ty felt comfortable enough with Toni to share her deepest secret. She shifted toward Toni, and then said, "Toni, I'm gonna share somethin' with you, and for now, I want you to keep it between us."

Toni hesitantly nodded, curious as to what Ty could be talking about. "If that's what you want," she assured her.

"Well, I, um…" Ty needed to calm her nerves, so she filled her lungs with kush smoke and then exhaled a thick cloud. She went on, "I recently found out that I have a brother, and it's Banks."

"Banks? How?" Toni was shocked and perplexed.

'Yes, apparently he and I have the same father. We found this out together when I went to visit my father's grave and Banks was there," she explained.

"You want me to keep this between us because you haven't told Diamond," Toni said in disbelief.

"I'm afraid it'll be too much for Diamond to deal with after all we've already been through. And Banks bein' my brother just makes things complicated," she stressed.

Toni sighed. "Ty, Banks has done things that are unforgivable and him bein' your brother won't change Diamond's heart. But neither will he have a change of heart about you. Listen, you need to tell Diamond soon because he should know."

"And I will," Ty assured her.

"Good." Toni grabbed the blunt from Ty's hand and said, "Yo' ass done blew a bitch high and shit." She took a deep drag of the weed. "Now let's turn up. Alexa play new Meg Thee Stallion on Amazon music," she instructed the device. Once the music came on she did a li'l twerk in her seat, causing Ty to shake her head and laugh.

***

Near closing time, Diamond decided to bounce from the club. Due to the escapade of the night of the reopening, as a precaution, Sarge and two others escorted Diamond out to his Bentley.

The streets were free of ice and Diamond zoomed the Bentley toward the condo, His iPhone chimed. Looking down at his phone in the cup holder, he noticed there was a text from Tywanna. He didn't bother to check the message since he'd be home soon. As Diamond zoomed down North Street, cop lights flashed behind him. Glancing up into the rearview mirror, he saw it was unmarked vehicle.

Muthafuckas always tryin' to catch a nigga ridin' dirty, Diamond contemplated with a dislike for the law. He veered to the curb and the vehicle followed. He pulled out his license and registration for the lawman, and if the car happened to be searched, then he wasn't concerned because his weapons were stashed in trap compartments. Once the officer had approached the driver's side, Diamond dashed down the window to hand over his plastic and pink slip to the cop. He then found himself staring down the barrel of a gun, and standing behind the trigger was Lynch!

"Outta the damn car," Lynch demanded. He pressed the barrel to Diamond's temple. "Now!"

Reluctantly, Diamond stepped out of the car. "What, you gonna arrest me on trumped up charges again? I may not have Levin to represent me anymore, since you offed him, but I'm confident yo' charges won't hold in court," he scoffed.

"Yeah, well, this time court will be held in the streets," Lynch said gruffly.

He frisked Diamond and found no weapon. After pressing a button, opening the Bentley's trunk, he practically dragged Diamond by the collar to the back of the vehicle. Lynch gave the trunk a quick search, and once finding no weapons there, he struck Diamond over the head with his pistol, forced him inside, then slammed the trunk shut.

A moment later, Diamond heard Lynch enter the Bentley before it drove off. Diamond's head was in pain, but all he was thinking was that he hoped Tywanna and Toni were safe. He understood that Lynch was planning to dead him, therefore Diamond had to do or die.

Some twenty miles outside of town, Lynch bent the car off road into a deserted wooded location. It was the best location for him to dump Diamond's corpse and vehicle, and it would be a very long time before either is found

Diamond felt the car come to a halt, and then a moment later, he heard Lynch getting out. Never did Diamond think he'd end up in a trunk with his life in danger, and he was prepared to die hard.

Stepping to the trunk with gun drawn, Lynch opened the trunk and to his dismay, he and Diamond were holding one another at gunpoint.

Blam, blam, blam!

Diamond's gun cracked thrice in a rapid succession, and slugs tore into the chest of Lynch. On impact, Lynch crumpled back into the dirt ground, and in a hurry, Diamond climbed out from the trunk. What Lynch didn't anticipate was that Diamond had a trap compartment concealing a gun inside the trunk of the Bentley.

Diamond didn't know where in the hell Lynch had brought him. In the spillover of the headlight beams, he saw that they were surrounded by woods, and he spotted a shovel and pile of dirt beside a prepared grave. He then glared down at Lynch along the barrel of the .32 revolver and growled, 'I don't appreciate you tryin' to dead me. But it's my pleasure to watch you die."

"We all die. It's just a question of when," Lynch grunted. He held his chest, his blood fountaining out between his fingers. "And I'm sure it won't be long for you and Frank."

"You know, I didn't realize how bad you have it for Balistrieri. And you were willin' to do any fuckin' thing to get rid of him. The ultimate betrayal," Diamond scoffed.

"For far too long I let that son of a bitch get away with blackmailing me to do his dirty work. I knew that the only justice I'd get would be that which I made myself, even if it meant obstructing the law." Lynch's breathing was labored.

"I'm sure Balistrieri will be pleased wit' your death as much as me," Diamond told him. "Now say your prayers, Lynch. But judgin' by you bein' a Judas, you won't be forgiven."

"Damn you, Diamond, only God can judge me!" Lynch cried out. He went into a coughing fit, and blood streamed down the corner of his mouth.

Diamond's eyes glittered coldly and he permitted himself a thin smile as he looked down on his victim. "I'm the Trap God."

Blam! Blam! Blam!

Diamond spent the second half of the rounds on Lynch, finishing him. He then grabbed the corpse by its ankles and dragged it over the dirt ground to the grave, then used a foot to shove the corpse into the hold in the ground. Grabbing the shovel, he began burying the corpse under dirt. Lynch had dug his own grave.

***

Upon entering the condo, Diamond found Tywanna standing on the coffee table dancing to the music and Toni on the love seat rolling up a blunt. He was grateful to see them both safe and sound. In that moment, he realized how much they shared his heart.

"Diamond, you're finally home," Ty said cheerfully.

"And just in time to blaze this blunt with us," Toni added, setting flames to the blunt.

Without words, Diamond leaned against the front door and slid down to the floor. He took a deep breath. Both girls hurried over to Diamond, noticing that there was dirt on his Balmain blue distressed jeans and on his brown leather Balmain Taiga boots. The girls helped him over to the love seat and sat on either on either side of him.

"Are you alright, Diamond?" Ty asked out of concern.

"What happened?" Toni cared to know.

Diamond grabbed the blunt and took a drag of the kush to ease his mind. "Yeah, I'm a'ight. But it's Lynch. He took me someplace wit' plans of leavin' me buried. Instead, I buried his ass never to be found," he told them. "Buryin' him, I couldn't help but think about how he tried to hurt both of you jus' to get to me. I wouldn't be able to live wit' myself if somethin' happens to either of you, especially if it's because of me. Because I love both of you more than myself," Diamond expressed.

"And we love you too, Diamond," Ty said.

"More than you know," Toni added.

Overcome by his feelings, Diamond kissed Tywanna passion-ately, then turned his head and kissed Toni just the same. Eventually they all engaged in a three-way kiss, each becoming undeniable aroused. Diamond hungered for both girls, but he wondered about Ty and her ability to handle being with him and another girl, espe-cially it being Toni.

Toni grabbed Ty's hand, pulled her to her feet, and now they stood before Diamond. Slowly and seductively, Toni unzipped Ty's Tom Ford mini dress and then pulled it off her, and in turn, Ty helped Toni out of her Chanel jersey dress. Both removed each other's lingerie. As the girls stood before him ass naked, Diamond caressed their bodies with his eyes. Both girls began stripping him out of his attire, Tywanna working on the top half and Toni on the bottom. Once Diamond was also ass naked, his hard, large dick stood at full length.

Ty commenced sucking Diamond's hardness, but Toni decided she wanted to also. So as they both licked their tongues up and down his dick, their tongues met. Diamond seemed to dig this, because pretty soon he pulled his dick away and Ty and Toni were left French-kissing. Toni reached down and stoked Ty's clit while she kissed her mouth. Ty's pussy was wet, the lips and clit swollen and satiny soft. She put her index and middle fingers inside Ty's wet shot, using her fingers to fuck her so slowly. She moved her fingers in and out, coating them with Ty's juices, and then put them in her own mouth. Diamond puffed the blunt as he watched Toni suck the juices from her fingers. She smiled up at him and did it again, scooping her wetness and giving him her fingers to suck. He sucked greedily, using his tongue as he did so.

Tywanna, Diamond noticed, seemed to be in almost a trance. She watched Toni through slitted eyes. Diamond sat on the love seat and watched Toni as she slowly began to seduce his girl. She stroked Ty gently on the shoulder, on the breasts, and up and down her legs. As she did, she put light kisses on Ty's neck, ears, and lips. Diamond found out not only could Ty handle it, she relished the touch of another girl.

After a few moments of foreplay, Toni had Tywanna on her back on the plush carpet. Her legs were splayed, her pussy was open, and her eyes were shut. Toni went to work on Ty's slit, licking it, sucking it, gently finger-fucking it. It didn't take long for Ty to have her first of many orgasms. Diamond savored the sight of his girl vibrating with erotic pleasure.

The girls climbed to their feet, each taking Diamond by a hand, and led him into the master bedroom, where they all crawled into bed and Diamond laid back. Toni straddled his head with her knees on the pillows. Diamond was stroking his dick as he watched Toni lower that juicy twat over his face. Ty straddled his hips and lowered her wet kitty toward his stiff cock. Watching Toni feed her man her pussy made Ty cum all over herself. Diamond's dick was rock-hard. Pre-cum oozed out the tip. Ty ducked her head and licked it up.

"I'm cummin'!" Toni suddenly cried. "Suck it, Diamond. Suck up every last drop!"

Diamond went wild. His tongue was everywhere. Toni arched her back, jamming her pussy on Diamond's mouth. They were lip to lip, and Ty could hear him sucking up Toni's cum. Both girls came all over Diamond.

"I wanna watch you eat her pussy. I wanna see you lick her juices," Diamond told Ty.

"Mmm'kay, baby," Ty cooed.

She was on her knees with her head buried in Toni's pussy, licking and sucking that good pussy, when she felt Diamond's hardness slide into her wet-wet from behind. His dick was hard, thick, and pulsating! She was making all kinds of slurping noises as Toni rubbed her pussy in her face. Diamond was really turned on watching her, and Toni was getting turned on watching him. Toni came all over Ty's face.

Suddenly Diamond pulled his piece out and shot warm nut all over Ty's ass. When Toni saw what Diamond had done, Ty saw a gleam in her eyes. Toni crawled behind Ty and started licking the nut from Ty's ass. Diamond stuck his love-tool deep into her gushy snatch. He dicked Toni as she licked the crease as well as Ty's asshole. While she massaged Ty with her tongue, her fingers was all over Ty's pussy, stroking her clit. Diamond came deep in Toni's slit as he brought her to orgasm, and Ty's cried of pleasure bounced off the walls.

Diamond sank back into the pillow as the girls lay down on either side of him. He kissed them both. "Damn, that was incredible. I appreciate havin' both of you in my life," he expressed.

Before he knew it, the girls were fast asleep. He lay there being soothed by their breathing. He loved them for separate reasons. Although he didn't know it, he loved one more than the other…

The next morning, daylight was attempting to make an indentation on the shadow of the bedroom. Diamond awakened, feeling only Tywanna in his arms. He slid out of bed and padded through the condo in search of Toni, discovering she slipped out while he was asleep. Returning to the bedroom, he sat on edge of the bed with his iPhone, intending to call Toni, when he noticed there was a text from her. Diamond read the message.

Toni// 7:42 a.m.
I didn't wanna leave, but it was best for you & Ty that I go.

Stirring awake, Tywanna said, "Morning, baby." She moved over to Diamond, wrapped her arms around his neck from behind, and kissed his cheek. "Where's Toni?"

"She had to go." Diamond understood Toni had only left to avoid a dilemma. But he wished she would have stayed.

Chapter 20

Tywanna placed a bouquet of flowers at the headstone of hers and Banks's father while he stood beside her. They decided to meet there to talk. Overhead the sun shone brightly, warming both land and people and melting all of the ice and snow as the summer season approached.

"I realize that I never knew our dad, but somehow I feel close to him," Ty said

"I feel you," Banks replied. "Oftentimes I wonder how life would be if he was here. Still can't believe that Tate, his closest friend, the man who raised me, had been the one who murdered him out of betrayal." His tone was a mixture of grief and anger.

"And how do you know he did it for sure?"

"He admitted to it when I confronted him. Also the part of ultimately bein' the case of my mother's overdose. And you know what he told me? The only thing he regrets is not killin' me." He shook his head and scoffed.

Ty placed a hand on his arm in solace and said, "That's awful. He deserves whatever he gets."

Bank brought his eyes to hers and remarked, "Which is why, deservingly enough, I gave his ass a fatal bullet."

"You did what you had to do, Banks," she replied, meaning it. "Listen, I'm sure it's not easy for you feelin' alone, so just know I'm here for you and only have your best interest at heart."

"I know. That's why I decided to take yo' word about Jade's claim. And it turns out you were right, she was not pregnant after all," he told her, sounding bitter.

Ty folded her arms, shifting her weight to one side. "To be honest with you, Banks, I'm not the least bit sorry that Jade isn't pregnant, on the strength of Lexi. Besides, how can someone like her even be a good mother to a childlike I would have been?" She shared in Banks's bitterness.

"Look, I know you're still dealin' wit' the loss of yo' child. Clearly she meant a lot to you. And you're right, Jade would never be as good of a mother as you'd be. Besides, I'd rather not have not have a li'l one wit' her on the strength of Lexi."

"For all I care, Jade can suffer," Ty said resentfully. She couldn't find it in her heart to feel remorse for Jade.

"Believe me, she's already sufferin'. Jade's now hooked on dope."

Ty shook her head. "I don't know what you ever saw in her. Or Gangsta, for that matter."

"Heard about what happened to Gangsta. Nigga got what he had comin'," Banks scoffed. "Jus' wish I was the one to fade his ass for what he did. Now part of me feels like he got away with' it." Hate glinted in his eyes.

"I know you feel that way because he was the one who killed Lex. I can never forgive Gangsta for it either, so I get how you feel."

"Not only did he kill Lex, but also our cousin Lucifer," Banks recalled in anger.

"Gangsta wasn't much to me, but I know how much he meant to Diamond. And that's why I try not to hate Gangsta, because he and Diamond were like brothers."

"I know." Banks was aware that Diamond and Gangsta had never given up on their brotherly love even with their differences. That was obvious the night they spared one another from him. He observed Ty and asked, "Speakin' of brothers, have you told Diamond about me bein' yours?"

Ty looked off into the distance. "I...I can't seem to bring myself to tell Diamond," she admitted.

"Listen, you really need to tell him. I'm sure he'll continue to love you jus' the same. And out of my love for you, I'm even willing to make a truce wit' Diamond," Banks told her.

Ty peered at him wide-eyed. "Really? You'd do that for me?"

"I just don't want you to get caught in between me and Diamond's problems."

Ty hugged him. "That means so much to me. And it makes it much easier for me to tell Diamond you're my brother." She drew back and met his eyes. "I don't wanna lose either of you due to one another, or have to take sides. Either would be painful."

***

Diamond cruised the Bentley through the cemetery. He was on his way to visit Chase's gravesite. It had been a while since he'd been there. In fact, he hadn't been there since he and Gangsta were there together. He remembered Chase telling him not to let the streets come in between him and Gangsta, and after all, Diamond abided. He hated that Chase and Gangsta had been lost to the streets, and he knew he had to get out of the streets before losing his own life. Because after the devastating loss of their unborn child, he wanted to be there for Tywanna. …

Diamond abruptly braked the Bentley once noticing Ty with Banks. They were standing in the graveyard, and he could only assume that Banks was trying to harm Ty to get even, and Diamond would protect her with his life. Without thinking twice, Diamond hurried out of the car and towards them.

"Get the fuck away from her!" Diamond demanded as he stepped up. He pulled Ty behind him.

"Diamond!" Ty was surprised by his presence.

"She has nothin' to do wit' me and your problems," he growled, mean-mugging Banks. "You better stay the fuck away from her, Banks."

"I can't do that, Diamond," Banks replied, struggling to hold his composure.

"You can and you will!" Diamond barked through clenched teeth.

Ty grabbed Diamond's arm, and cried, "Diamond wait!"

Whop!

Diamond took off on Banks, hammering him on the jaw and causing him to stumble backwards. And then Banks countered with a flurry of fists, connecting to his face. As the two threw hands, Ty pleaded for them to stop fighting, but to no avail. Witnessing her lover and her brother attempt to beat one another to a bloody pulp pulled Ty's heart and her mind in opposite directions. She struggled with how to feel and what to do. After tussling a bit, Diamond and

Banks ended up on the ground at the feet of Tywanna, both men going at one another. As Ty attempted to break them up, she was knocked onto the ground.

"Please, stop!" Ty cried despairingly. "Diamond, Banks is my brother!"

Suddenly Diamond stopped, he looked over at Ty in disbelief. But Banks seized the moment to flip Diamond onto his back and then straddled his torso, clamping his hands around Diamond's throat.

Ty wasn't willing to let Banks choke Diamond to death. She scrambled for her Prada purse and came out with her .380 handgun. She squeezed the trigger.

Bang!

To Be Continued...
Trap God 3
Coming Soon

Submission Guideline

Submit the first three chapters of your completed manuscript to ldpsubmissions@gmail.com, subject line: Your book's title. The manuscript must be in a .doc file and sent as an attachment. Document should be in Times New Roman, double spaced and in size 12 font. Also, provide your synopsis and full contact information. If sending multiple submissions, they must each be in a separate email.

Have a story but no way to send it electronically? You can still submit to LDP/Ca$h Presents. Send in the first three chapters, written or typed, of your completed manuscript to:

LDP: Submissions Dept
Po Box 944
Stockbridge, Ga 30281

DO NOT send original manuscript. Must be a duplicate.

Provide your synopsis and a cover letter containing your full contact information.

Thanks for considering LDP and Ca$h Presents.

Coming Soon from Lock Down Publications/Ca$h Presents

BOW DOWN TO MY GANGSTA
By **Ca$h**
TORN BETWEEN TWO
By **Coffee**
THE STREETS STAINED MY SOUL **II**
By **Marcellus Allen**
BLOOD OF A BOSS **VI**
SHADOWS OF THE GAME II
By **Askari**
LOYAL TO THE GAME **IV**
By **T.J. & Jelissa**
A DOPEBOY'S PRAYER **II**
By **Eddie "Wolf" Lee**
IF LOVING YOU IS WRONG… **III**
By **Jelissa**
TRUE SAVAGE **VII**
MIDNIGHT CARTEL III
DOPE BOY MAGIC IV
CITY OF KINGZ II
By **Chris Green**
BLAST FOR ME **III**
A SAVAGE DOPEBOY III
CUTTHROAT MAFIA III
By **Ghost**
A HUSTLER'S DECEIT III
KILL ZONE **II**
BAE BELONGS TO ME III
A DOPE BOY'S QUEEN III

By **Aryanna**

COKE KINGS V

KING OF THE TRAP II

By **T.J. Edwards**

GORILLAZ IN THE BAY V

De'Kari

THE STREETS ARE CALLING II

Duquie Wilson

KINGPIN KILLAZ IV

STREET KINGS III

PAID IN BLOOD III

CARTEL KILLAZ IV

DOPE GODS III

Hood Rich

SINS OF A HUSTLA II

ASAD

KINGZ OF THE GAME V

Playa Ray

SLAUGHTER GANG IV

RUTHLESS HEART IV

By **Willie Slaughter**

THE HEART OF A SAVAGE III

By **Jibril Williams**

FUK SHYT II

By **Blakk Diamond**

THE REALEST KILLAZ II

By **Tranay Adams**

TRAP GOD III

By **Troublesome**

YAYO IV

A SHOOTER'S AMBITION III

By S. Allen

GHOST MOB

Stilloan Robinson

KINGPIN DREAMS III

By Paper Boi Rari

CREAM

By Yolanda Moore

SON OF A DOPE FIEND III

By Renta

FOREVER GANGSTA II

GLOCKS ON SATIN SHEETS III

By Adrian Dulan

LOYALTY AIN'T PROMISED II

By Keith Williams

THE PRICE YOU PAY FOR LOVE II

DOPE GIRL MAGIC III

By Destiny Skai

CONFESSIONS OF A GANGSTA II

By Nicholas Lock

I'M NOTHING WITHOUT HIS LOVE II

By Monet Dragun

LIFE OF A SAVAGE IV

A GANGSTA'S QUR'AN II

MURDA SEASON II

By **Romell Tukes**

QUIET MONEY III

THUG LIFE II

By **Trai'Quan**

THE STREETS MADE ME III

By **Larry D. Wright**
THE ULTIMATE SACRIFICE VI
IF YOU CROSS ME ONCE II
ANGEL III
By **Anthony Fields**
THE LIFE OF A HOOD STAR
By **Ca$h & Rashia Wilson**
FRIEND OR FOE II
By **Mimi**
SAVAGE STORMS II
By **Meesha**
BLOOD ON THE MONEY II
By J-Blunt

Available Now

RESTRAINING ORDER **I & II**
By **CA$H & Coffee**
LOVE KNOWS NO BOUNDARIES **I II & III**
By **Coffee**
RAISED AS A GOON I, II, III & IV
BRED BY THE SLUMS I, II, III
BLAST FOR ME I & II
ROTTEN TO THE CORE I II III
A BRONX TALE I, II, III
DUFFEL BAG CARTEL I II III IV

Troublesome

HEARTLESS GOON I II III IV
A SAVAGE DOPEBOY I II
HEARTLESS GOON I II III
DRUG LORDS I II III
CUTTHROAT MAFIA I II
By **Ghost**
LAY IT DOWN **I & II**
LAST OF A DYING BREED
BLOOD STAINS OF A SHOTTA I & II III
By **Jamaica**
LOYAL TO THE GAME I II III
LIFE OF SIN I, II III
By **TJ & Jelissa**
BLOODY COMMAS I & II
SKI MASK CARTEL I II & III
KING OF NEW YORK I II,III IV V
RISE TO POWER I II III
COKE KINGS I II III IV
BORN HEARTLESS I II III IV
KING OF THE TRAP
By **T.J. Edwards**
IF LOVING HIM IS WRONG…I & II
LOVE ME EVEN WHEN IT HURTS I II III
By **Jelissa**
WHEN THE STREETS CLAP BACK I & II III
THE HEART OF A SAVAGE I II
By **Jibril Williams**
A DISTINGUISHED THUG STOLE MY HEART I II & III
LOVE SHOULDN'T HURT I II III IV
RENEGADE BOYS I II III IV

198

PAID IN KARMA I II III

SAVAGE STORMS

By **Meesha**

A GANGSTER'S CODE I &, II III

A GANGSTER'S SYN I II III

THE SAVAGE LIFE I II III

CHAINED TO THE STREETS I II III

BLOOD ON THE MONEY

By J-Blunt

PUSH IT TO THE LIMIT

By **Bre' Hayes**

BLOOD OF A BOSS **I, II, III, IV, V**

SHADOWS OF THE GAME

By **Askari**

THE STREETS BLEED MURDER **I, II & III**

THE HEART OF A GANGSTA I II& III

By **Jerry Jackson**

CUM FOR ME I II III IV V

An **LDP Erotica Collaboration**

BRIDE OF A HUSTLA **I II & II**

THE FETTI GIRLS **I, II& III**

CORRUPTED BY A GANGSTA I, II III, IV

BLINDED BY HIS LOVE

THE PRICE YOU PAY FOR LOVE

DOPE GIRL MAGIC I II

By **Destiny Skai**

WHEN A GOOD GIRL GOES BAD

By **Adrienne**

THE COST OF LOYALTY I II III

By Kweli

A GANGSTER'S REVENGE **I II III & IV**

THE BOSS MAN'S DAUGHTERS I II III IV V

A SAVAGE LOVE **I & II**

BAE BELONGS TO ME I II

A HUSTLER'S DECEIT I, II, III

WHAT BAD BITCHES DO I, II, III

SOUL OF A MONSTER I II III

KILL ZONE

A DOPE BOY'S QUEEN I II

By **Aryanna**

A KINGPIN'S AMBITON

A KINGPIN'S AMBITION **II**

I MURDER FOR THE DOUGH

By **Ambitious**

TRUE SAVAGE I II III IV V VI

DOPE BOY MAGIC I, II, III

MIDNIGHT CARTEL I II

CITY OF KINGZ

By **Chris Green**

A DOPEBOY'S PRAYER

By **Eddie "Wolf" Lee**

THE KING CARTEL **I, II & III**

By **Frank Gresham**

THESE NIGGAS AIN'T LOYAL **I, II & III**

By **Nikki Tee**

GANGSTA SHYT **I II &III**

By **CATO**

THE ULTIMATE BETRAYAL

By **Phoenix**

BOSS'N UP **I , II & III**

By **Royal Nicole**

I LOVE YOU TO DEATH

By Destiny J

I RIDE FOR MY HITTA

I STILL RIDE FOR MY HITTA

By **Misty Holt**

LOVE & CHASIN' PAPER

By **Qay Crockett**

TO DIE IN VAIN

SINS OF A HUSTLA

By **ASAD**

BROOKLYN HUSTLAZ

By **Boogsy Morina**

BROOKLYN ON LOCK I & II

By **Sonovia**

GANGSTA CITY

By **Teddy Duke**

A DRUG KING AND HIS DIAMOND I & II III

A DOPEMAN'S RICHES

HER MAN, MINE'S TOO I, II

CASH MONEY HO'S

By Nicole Goosby

TRAPHOUSE KING **I II & III**

KINGPIN KILLAZ I II III

STREET KINGS I II

PAID IN BLOOD **I II**

CARTEL KILLAZ I II III

DOPE GODS I II

By **Hood Rich**

LIPSTICK KILLAH **I, II, III**

Troublesome

CRIME OF PASSION I II & III

FRIEND OR FOE

By **Mimi**

STEADY MOBBN' **I, II, III**

THE STREETS STAINED MY SOUL

By **Marcellus Allen**

WHO SHOT YA **I, II, III**

SON OF A DOPE FIEND I II

Renta

GORILLAZ IN THE BAY **I II III IV**

TEARS OF A GANGSTA I II

DE'KARI

TRIGGADALE I II III

Elijah R. Freeman

GOD BLESS THE TRAPPERS I, II, III

THESE SCANDALOUS STREETS I, II, III

FEAR MY GANGSTA I, II, III IV, V

THESE STREETS DON'T LOVE NOBODY I, II

BURY ME A G I, II, III, IV, V

A GANGSTA'S EMPIRE I, II, III, IV

THE DOPEMAN'S BODYGAURD I II

THE REALEST KILLAZ

Tranay Adams

THE STREETS ARE CALLING

Duquie Wilson

MARRIED TO A BOSS... I II III

By **Destiny Skai & Chris Green**

KINGZ OF THE GAME I II III IV

Playa Ray

SLAUGHTER GANG I II III

RUTHLESS HEART I II III
By Willie Slaughter
FUK SHYT
By Blakk Diamond
DON'T F#CK WITH MY HEART I II
By Linnea
ADDICTED TO THE DRAMA I II III
By Jamila
YAYO I II III
A SHOOTER'S AMBITION I II
By S. Allen
TRAP GOD I II
By Troublesome
FOREVER GANGSTA
GLOCKS ON SATIN SHEETS I II
By Adrian Dulan
TOE TAGZ I II III
By Ah'Million
KINGPIN DREAMS I II
By Paper Boi Rari
CONFESSIONS OF A GANGSTA
By Nicholas Lock
I'M NOTHING WITHOUT HIS LOVE
By Monet Dragun
CAUGHT UP IN THE LIFE I II III
By Robert Baptiste
NEW TO THE GAME I II III
By **Malik D. Rice**
LIFE OF A SAVAGE I II III
A GANGSTA'S QUR'AN

MURDA SEASON

By **Romell Tukes**

LOYALTY AIN'T PROMISED

By Keith Williams

QUIET MONEY I II

THUG LIFE

By **Trai'Quan**

THE STREETS MADE ME I II

By **Larry D. Wright**

THE ULTIMATE SACRIFICE I, II, III, IV, V

KHADIFI

IF YOU CROSS ME ONCE

ANGEL I II

By **Anthony Fields**

THE LIFE OF A HOOD STAR

By Ca$h & Rashia Wilson

BOOKS BY LDP'S CEO, CA$H

TRUST IN NO MAN

TRUST IN NO MAN 2

TRUST IN NO MAN 3

BONDED BY BLOOD

SHORTY GOT A THUG

THUGS CRY

THUGS CRY 2

THUGS CRY 3

TRUST NO BITCH

TRUST NO BITCH 2

TRUST NO BITCH 3

TIL MY CASKET DROPS

RESTRAINING ORDER

RESTRAINING ORDER 2

IN LOVE WITH A CONVICT

LIFE OF A HOOD STAR

Coming Soon

BONDED BY BLOOD 2

BOW DOWN TO MY GANGSTA

Troublesome

www.ingramcontent.com/pod-product-compliance
Lightning Source LLC
Chambersburg PA
CBHW070503260626
47161CB00004B/1430